Impressing
Jeanette

Impressing Jeanette

A Novel by
Adrian Robert Gostick

Bookcraft
Salt Lake City, Utah

Library of Congress Catalog Card Number: 97-72348
ISBN 1-57008-324-X

First Printing, 1997

Printed in the United States of America

For Anthony

Thanks to Janet Thomas, Richard Romney, Larry Hiller, and the staff of the *New Era* magazine; to my coworkers who bought copies of *Eddy and the Habs* as I sat alone at my first book signing; and to Jennifer.

All characters in this book are fictitious,
and any resemblance to actual persons,
living or dead, is purely coincidental.

— CHAPTER 1 —

Tony

Spring Valley, Montana, population 12,148, lies in a wintry, wheaty stretch of rolling hills and valleys forty-five miles out of Great Falls toward the Canadian border. This is railroad country, where we tell time by the high-pitched locomotive whistles that resound around the city like distant ghosts.

Except for maybe when the rails were first put in, a hundred years before, I can think of only one other big milestone in the history of our town: the construction of the Spring Valley High School.

The high school is probably the ugliest school in the state, looking suspiciously like the local IGA supermarket. In fact, it's nothing more than a gigantic shoe box with a loading dock at the back. The building itself is not significant, but what happened after it arrived. In the ten years after Principal Walker welcomed grades nine through twelve to the first classes held in the school, a burgeoning metropolis sprang up in Spring Valley. And most importantly, a couple of gas stations with food marts opened.

My family was there before the school. So we were locals.

However, about half the population of Spring Valley arrived after the school. And thus they were newcomers.

And while every family that moved to Spring Valley in the years following the school's construction were considered newcomers, no people better fit the title than Paul and Leona Burhold.

The Burholds arrived in town with a dark cloud of mystery surrounding them. Most of that mystery stemmed from the fact that no one knew what they did for a living. No one ever saw Paul or Leona Burhold go to a job. As far as anyone knew, they hardly ever left town. So the source of their income was an item of great interest to us locals. They had enough money to drive a Mercedes, so obviously they got money from somewhere. But they lived in Spring Valley, so they were either hiding from the law or they were really, really dumb.

The weeks passed, and they said nothing about their jobs and very little about their lives before Spring Valley. In fact, for the first few weeks all they did was ask questions, lots of strange, probing questions.

Then, while still unpacking at their big ranch house on the north edge of town, Leona volunteered at the local hospital and Paul at the fire department. After that, they volunteered with a vengeance. They were everywhere. When you went to a ward party, they were setting up chairs or arranging the bowls of carrot-filled Jell-O. When you went to the ice rink, they were selling hot dogs or scraping the ice. If someone was shoveling his drive, Paul Burhold was always there, throwing shovelfuls of the wet powder like it was Styrofoam and sweating like he was a sprinkler.

I hated the way they always smiled, the way they always waved at you, the fact they were so nice all the time. They tried so hard to be likeable that we all knew something wasn't right about them.

And something wasn't.

But we'll get to the Burholds soon enough. First I have to tell you about their son, Tony.

And we should probably start at the beginning.

———

We'd heard that a new kid was coming.

It was early one December Wednesday, and we were taking turns reading aloud from *Moby Dick* as Mrs. Curry, our English teacher, stared out the gray window, swaying back and forth as if she were standing on the bow of a whaling ship.

I was reading when Principal Walker's voice crackled over the intercom.

"New . . . umm . . . student, Mrs. Curry," he said slowly. Then for a moment we listened to his troubled breathing until finally he muttered, "Not what we expected," and the intercom went dead.

We all looked at each other and then at the hallway.

Eventually we heard footsteps—Principal Walker in his patent-leather shoes—and then suddenly there were two figures in the doorway: Principal Walker and the new kid.

And he was not, I'm sure, what *anyone* had expected.

Usually we got cowboy-boot-wearing farm kids with bad haircuts. At the most exotic, a zit-faced town kid in cheap high-tops.

But this guy wasn't a typical, awkward sixteen-year-old. His dark hair was styled, his face was clear, and he wore expensive-looking clothes. He was tall, taller than Walker by about half a foot. He had a square jaw and wide shoulders, and under his leather jacket he had a chest the diameter of an oil drum. His face was handsome, I guess, except for a dark ridge of scary eyebrows too thick and brown for his features.

Principal Walker moved through the door, and the new kid followed. Mrs. Curry had been leaning against a wall trying to look casual, but when Principal Walker glared in her direction she sprang to life and grabbed the kid's arm. She walked him down an aisle, and then when they were in front of an empty desk she bent at the knees and did some kind of dramatic sweep with both hands.

I'd never seen Mrs. Curry act so goofy.

Principal Walker and Mrs. Curry regrouped by the door as the kid squeezed his large frame into one of our smaller desks.

"Mercedes," Walker whispered to Curry, nodding in the guy's direction. Principal Walker never spoke in complete sentences.

"He drives a Mercedes?" Curry echoed in disbelief.

"No," said Walker, folding his arms. "Parents."

A few guys who could hear them made impressed noises. As usual, Principal Walker glared at me to shut up. He thought I was an idiot.

"Tell us your name and where you're from," said Mrs. Curry, standing at the head of the kid's row and holding her hands together as if she were praying.

But the new kid didn't answer right away. Instead, he cooly, slowly pulled off his leather jacket to reveal forearms lined with rippling muscles that looked like little mountain ranges on a globe.

Then he said, "Tony Burhold. I was born in Manhattan. That's in New York." All the girls laughed, though I had no idea why.

Even Mrs. Curry clapped her hands together and laughed. Mrs. Curry had a wide, wide mouth that grew absolutely immense when she opened it to laugh—she looked like a really big Pez dispenser.

"Yes," said Mrs. Curry, almost singing, "we're not *that* provincial. Did your parents get work around here? Is that why you moved?"

"Uh, I guess you could say that."

I looked back at Jeanette McCaffrey to see if she had laughed along with Mrs. Curry and the other girls. She hadn't. In fact, she was picking her fingernails, ignoring the new guy.

Jeanette McCaffrey was, without doubt, better looking than any other girl I knew. She had long, thick copper-colored hair that swung back and forth like soft wheat moving in the wind. She had skin the color of expensive vanilla ice cream. And her green eyes were framed by long, dark eyelashes, which now and then would clump together like a Raggedy Ann doll's—but even that looked good.

She was the closest thing to an egghead we had in school. For the tenth grade science fair, Jeanette created a working model of something called a passive-solar house. Principal Walker gave her the blue ribbon, though it was obvious he didn't understand half the equations Jeanette had scribbled around the edges of the little house.

She also was a football cheerleader, hung with the coolest kids, and did a lot of other stuff that made her popular. But probably the main reason I found her so irresistible was what she didn't do. She didn't talk to me, she didn't smile at me, she didn't even acknowledge that I was alive. She ignored me more completely than she ignored any other guy in school.

I'd known Jeanette for years. She even lived on the same road I did. We saw each other every school day and most Sundays at church. But we never spoke. The times I'd finally build up enough courage to say something to her, I'd end up doing something really embarrassing before I got my first word out.

One time I sat down next to her in the cafeteria. Before starting in on my carefully rehearsed, spontaneous conversation, I opened a can of root beer. It exploded, spraying my head and making my hair stand up straight all afternoon. Another time I walked into Sunday School determined to break the ice with Jeanette before the teacher opened her mouth. Of course, after I was told I had a line of toothpaste drool down the front of my green tie, I lost my nerve.

Eventually, I gave up the idea of ever talking to Jeanette.

When she turned sixteen, Jeanette went to work after school at a café in town. I would come home late after basketball practice and walk slowly by the café, hoping to catch a glimpse of her. My older brother, Matt, who was a senior, told me I was an idiot not to ask Jeanette out. He said everyone in school knew I had a crush on her. But I still couldn't bring myself to do anything about it.

Somehow I couldn't convince my tongue or my sweat glands to cooperate. When I saw Jeanette, all I could think about was how tall and skinny I was, how my face wouldn't clear up, or how just at the wrong moment my voice sounded like the noise you make when you blow a saxophone wrong.

And then Tony Burhold and his vacant blue eyes showed up in class. And an all-encompassing jealousy swept over me. Jeanette was ignoring another guy! All was lost.

I hated Tony Burhold.

———

That afternoon Tony tried out for our varsity basketball team.

Well, to be honest no one had ever tried out for our team. The state rules said we could have twelve guys on the roster, but each year we had only eight or nine show up for fall tryouts. So anyone who wanted to play made it.

Partly because of those slim pickings, our team had won only a handful of our games that season. Most humiliating was a 48–46 loss to Grover Cleveland *Junior* High in Helena. Grover Cleveland was a huge school with hundreds of kids. But still, it was a *junior* high! When Principal Walker announced the game's results over the loudspeaker, my class didn't stop laughing for a full five minutes.

But we were the only varsity boys basketball team in Spring Valley High School, and that afternoon we strode onto the court in front of the waiting Tony Burhold like we owned the place. Coach gathered the team around with a sweep of his hairy arm, then he squeezed Tony's muscular shoulder.

"Boys, this is Tony Burhold. I think we'll scrimmage a little today." Coach was using his deepest voice, sounding, I'd imagine, much like an air traffic controller giving a 747 permission to land.

"Starters play reserves," he added with equal authority.

Actually, Coach didn't know any plays. All we *ever* did was scrimmage.

"Tony, since you're a tall drink of water, I'm going to play you at center on the reserve squad," Coach said. "Let's see what you can do." Then Coach tossed Tony the ball.

The ball seemed to fly in slow motion as Tony opened one of his hands, which were about as wide as a Sizzler salad plate, and *thud*—he palmed the thing. He stopped a regulation basketball dead in midair with one hand! Our collective mouths dropped open. We'd never had anyone on our team who could do that.

"Eeeow," said Coach quietly, sounding like a cat. Then he collected his composure. "Okay, boys. Let's jump." He cautiously took the ball back from Tony.

I hadn't realized until that moment that as the starting center it was my job to jump against Tony and to defend Tony. I looked over, and he flexed his biceps. *Gulp.*

We lined up, and I shook off my fear. I'd defend him hard, even though I'd have to give him the tip-off without contest. I just knew that was a lost cause. My vertical jump was a sorry, sorry thing. Somehow gravity had a much stronger hold on me than on most guys. In fact, they'd made me center only because I was a couple of inches taller than anyone else on the team.

When I was younger, like about fourteen, I remember praying every night for God to let my athletic ability catch up with my height, to let me wake up one morning with a lightning first step like Jordan or a never-miss jump shot like Bird. But it never happened. In time I kind of came to accept my inability on the court. Anyway, our team was so bad that no girls from school ever came to our games, so no one except the guys on the team knew I dribbled with the coordination of a village idiot.

Unfortunately, my extremely mediocre abilities were not uncommon on the Spring Valley High team. We were all pretty average. But while we were all mediocre, we'd have been a lot better if we had any sort of coaching at all. Our coach's only regular valuable contribution to our betterment as players was repeated when he stood between Tony and me and threw the ball into the air.

I stood still while Tony jumped and tipped the ball back to Chris, our reserve point guard. Chris faked left then veered right, bringing the ball up the edge of the court. He looked for openings inside and then outside, but as usual most of the reserves weren't open or were looking in the wrong direction. Tony, however, had posted up on me in the lane. He was waving his arms for the ball. So Chris fed a neat bounce pass into him.

Tony was ten feet from the basket, but I had him boxed out. So Tony twisted, faded to the right, and jumped. I went up too, determined to swat the ball into the stands, but before I got six inches off the hardwood Tony's shot was arching high over my arms. *Swish*.

The reserve squad cheered like they had won the game. Actually, they had good reason to cheer. They rarely scored so quickly or so easily during our scrimmages. But I wasn't about to get excited for them. I was mad.

"Get back on defense, you meatheads," Coach yelled at the reserves, rubbing his shiny scalp.

They ran after us, but we were already at their basket. Steve scored a simple left-handed layup, and Tony inbounded to Chris, who again brought the ball up-court.

Ben was wide-open this time as our new star reserve was being triple-teamed. But it was obvious Chris wasn't going to pass to anyone but Tony Burhold. So Chris backed off, then brought the ball in again, all the time keeping his eyes fixed on Tony. Still, I and the entire starting front line were glued to Tony. Finally Chris gave up and lobbed a prayer of a pass into the crowd of out-stretched arms in the lane. I was about to jump when I felt an iron elbow in my ribs. Suddenly I was on the ground gasping for breath. I looked up, hoping that somebody, anybody, would beat Tony Burhold to the ball. Of course, he jumped higher than everyone.

But while everyone else fell to the earth, a slave to gravity, Tony didn't. Instead he grabbed the ball and turned in midair. Using his momentum, he let fly a pretty hook shot over the stunned starters. The ball hit the edge of the rim and rolled around and around for a few seconds. Tony didn't wait to see if it would drop. Instead, he pushed through the crowd and waited a couple of feet from the basket, ready to grab his own rebound when it rolled off the rim. This time he snagged the ball, came back to earth, and then prepared to drive the lane.

I was up by this time, sucking in air through my mouth but ready to defend the basket. Tony saw me and charged. I stood my ground. This was it. I'd show him.

Our bodies met, and for a second I flew through the sweaty gymnasium air. But my 150 pounds didn't slow Tony's ascent. In what seemed like slow motion, he rose higher and higher until he was above the rim. Then he slammed the ball through the hoop. The rim rocked violently after Tony let go and dropped back to the floor.

All of us, the starters and reserves, stood in shock. As far as I could recall, no one at Spring Valley had ever slam-dunked a basketball in a game or scrimmage. A few of our taller players, including me, could touch the rim while we fooled around before practice, but we needed a full run. Tony stuffed the ball. And he did it within his first few minutes on our team!

Nobody came to see if I was okay. In fact, Coach and the other players spent the next few seconds patting Tony on the back. They wanted to touch the guy, to make sure he was real. But Tony didn't smile or thank them for their compliments, he just nodded as if to say it was about time they realized who he was. He was Tony Burhold, and he'd arrived to lead Spring Valley High School from the miserable wasteland of its basketball past.

I pushed myself off the floor. "Oh brother," I mumbled as I rolled my eyes. But then I realized that Tony had seen me standing alone, not part of his adoring crowd. And he'd seen my look of disgust. He kept nodding, but I knew he'd drawn a conclusion about me.

I knew then that Tony Burhold hated me too.

————

That Thursday, Tony took my spot in the lineup at an away game against Havre. As I sat on the bench, our new center effortlessly scored twenty-four points and grabbed about a dozen rebounds to lead Spring Valley to our first blowout victory in a long time.

On Friday, Tony Burhold instantly became something our school had rarely seen: a real sports hero. The school's female population stood in the halls and giggled in admiration as he walked by. The girls must have realized he was about as bright as a box of rocks, but they didn't seem to care. Tony would pepper his conversations with phrases such as, "Cold out, huh?" and any girl around him would laugh and grin like she was showing off new teeth.

And then, as if Tony weren't satisfied just stealing all the attention at school, when we got to early-morning seminary the next morning Tony was there. He was a Mormon!

————

My brother, Matt, and I always sat on the back row during seminary, the only row where you could really stretch your legs out and lean your head back against the wall.

Tony walked into the classroom and took a seat at the back on the other side of the room from us.

Then Brother Fuggle-Hensley started his lesson. Yes, that was really his name, Fuggle-Hensley. He'd come from Germany as a young boy. He'd married his wife in Utah while he was still in college. Then after much fasting and prayer—we were told every week—he'd decided to pursue the puritan life as a seminary teacher. Three children followed. Three little girls forced to go through life with names the Fuggle-Hensleys had gleaned from the most remote corners of their imagination. Of the three girls, Liberty Belle Fuggle-Hensley was the oldest. Then came Kismet Canterbury Fuggle-Hensley, and then Rain Showers Fuggle-Hensley.

Brother Fuggle-Hensley was droning on and on. I glanced over every now and then at Tony, whose simple mind quickly lost interest. He leaned forward, putting his head on his desk. Within ten minutes, it was obvious Tony was asleep. His bearish back rose and fell slowly. I nudged Matt, and he looked over and snickered.

I wasn't watching when it happened, but I heard the sound. Tony in his relaxed state had leaned too far forward, and his whole desk had toppled over, the top of his head hitting the hardwood floor with a resounding *bonk!* Instantly the back desks started shaking violently as we tried to hold our laughter. Matt and I looked at each other and couldn't hold it in.

"Ha, ha, ha—snort," laughed Matt through his nose.

Brother Fuggle-Hensley, who never tolerated or even understood the need for humor, looked down the aisle furiously. That shut us up.

———

But that bonk on the head was the only flaw in Tony's shining armor. Even then, Tony didn't suffer. As word spread to the girls of Spring Valley, his accident somehow made him less scary and more human, even vulnerable.

— CHAPTER 2 —

First Impressings

On a Tuesday night in February, Matt and I were doing homework upstairs in my room. Well, I was doing homework, Matt was filling out sweepstakes forms. We got at least a dozen forms in the mail every week, and Matt filled them out religiously, never buying anything they offered but putting the stamps in all the right places. After a chuckle, Matt looked up from a form splashed with purple and black ink that told us we should begin ordering the popular book series *Life in America's Small Towns* because we could win an $82,000 BMW 850 or a four-day trip to the Super Bowl. What would we do with an $82,000 luxury car in Spring Valley?

"Ha," he said, looking at me.

"What're you ha-ing at?" I asked.

"Oh, nothing."

"You're just spontaneously ha-ing now?"

"I just thought you'd be interested in something. Aw, but it's nothing."

"What?"

"I saw someone giving Jeanette a ride home last night. Told you it was nothing."

"What do I care?" I said, as nonchalantly as possible, my guts tightening with each passing breath.

He shrugged and turned back to his sweepstakes form. He licked the stamp for the $1,000 early-entry prize and carefully placed it above the stamp for the Super Bowl holiday.

I couldn't take it any longer. "Okay, who?"

"That new guy," said Matt.

"Tony? Tony Burhold?"

"Yeah. That's the guy. Good-looking but kind of scary. Nice Mercedes."

My heart stopped. I pictured Jeanette riding in the Burholds' gold Mercedes, laughing at any stupid thing the doofus said. Tony would probably try the old yawn trick and put his big ape arm around her. They'd be engaged by the weekend.

"You waited too long," said Matt, grinning. He put his thumb on the $1,000 stamp again, to make sure it was affixed properly. "The new guy got to her first."

"You don't *get* to a girl like Jeanette," I snapped back.

"Well, *you* didn't."

"Just because he took her home once doesn't mean they're going out—does it?"

Matt shrugged. "I don't know. But I'd still ask her out if I were you. You've got nothing to lose. And if you don't, you'll regret it."

I swallowed at the thought of asking Jeanette out. First, I'd have to talk to her. And then, Tony would probably kill me.

"Aw, what do you know?"

I wasn't about to take Matt's advice. After all, I reminded myself, this was the guy who'd gotten me kicked out of Scouts when I was twelve, after only a month in the troop.

I'd joined Scouts only because most of the guys in my class had. Matt said Scouting was for conformists, whatever that meant, and wouldn't join with me.

So there I was, in my first full assembly—you know, parents and loved ones in the audience, all beaming with pride. And I was sitting with my patrol, the Falcons.

"Geez, what kind of Falcon are you?" Matt whispered from the row behind, where the civilians were seated. "I'd do it, if *I* was a Falcon," he added.

I could hear him settle back into his seat, but I knew his eyes were fixed on the back of my head. I wasn't going to turn around. No way. Beads of sweat began dripping around my ear and falling onto my crisp uniform. Still, I refused to wipe them away. Somehow I just couldn't show Matt I was alive.

I heard him lean forward again, and I stiffened.

"You know I'm right," he said softly, over my shoulder.

I couldn't resist. I turned around and looked into my older brother's nodding, melon-shaped face. His eyebrows were lowered —thoughtful, sincere.

And I was lost.

It made sense. After all, the patrol I had been put in was more than Scouts, we were *Falcons*. And since I was so new in the troop, I needed to make a big impression. So I reluctantly shrugged, and Matt settled back into his chair again. He knew I'd do it.

It's important to note that Jeanette McCaffrey was in the audience to watch one of her younger brothers. I rationalized that Matt's idea would probably impress her.

"New boy in Falcon patrol," said Principal Walker, who was not only the principal but the scoutmaster, a city councilman, a volunteer firefighter, president of the Valley Lodge, and a few other important things.

"Andrew, present patrol flag," he continued.

At that cue, I was supposed to stand up and ceremoniously lead our patrol to the head of the auditorium while holding the Falcon flag in one hand. But acting on Matt's advice, I put the flag in my teeth and began to flap my arms up and down and scream "caaaaaw, caaaaaw!" like a bird as I hopped in front of my stunned patrol.

Principal Walker's mouth dropped open, but the rest of the audience burst into hysterical laughter. They didn't stop for a long, long time. And while they laughed, Principal Walker's face turned redder and redder until it was the color of red twirly licorice.

———

"Do I really look stupid enough to listen to you?" I asked, breaking away from the bad memory. "Anyway, you don't just ask a girl like Jeanette out. It's not that easy."

Matt sat up on the edge of his bed and pushed the sweepstakes forms under his pillow. "Fine, don't listen, Chucklehead. But Tony doesn't own the girl. He can't do anything about it if she chooses you."

"Except beat me up."

"He's not going to beat you up."

"Right. He already hates me."

"Well, wouldn't it be worth a little pain if you got to go out with Jeanette? Or if you got to kiss Jeanette?"

"Hmmm, maybe." He was starting to win me over.

"Anyway, you're not asking the girl to get married. You're just going to drive her home, maybe ask her to a movie. This really isn't rocket science. It's just for fun. And you've got a lot to talk about. You're both in the same grade at school, have the same teachers, go to the same ward, both live in Spring Valley, know the same people. And if you run out of stuff to say, just talk about me. I'm a great conversation topic."

Matt may have led me astray in the past, but what he was saying actually made sense. I'd worried about dating Jeanette for years. But he was right, dating wasn't supposed to be stressful. It was supposed to be fun.

"So how would *you* do it?" I asked, still retaining my cynical tone. "I mean, how would you ask her out? I can't compete with Tony's vehicle or his looks."

"I don't know," said Matt. "But I wouldn't look at everything that was wrong with the situation. I'd look at everything that was right. I'd think about what I have to offer and not what I don't have."

I put my book down and laid back on my pillow, listening to the wind whistle around the edge of the house. Matt pulled his forms out again and went back to licking stamps.

I thought about Jeanette McCaffrey and what I could do to really impress her.

————

The next afternoon after basketball practice I passed the café where Jeanette worked. Of course, I did that every afternoon. But this day was going to be different. I was going to go inside the Shamrock. I was going to talk to gorgeous Jeanette McCaffrey.

Tom and Gwen Daugherty had built the Shamrock Café in 1947 after arriving in Spring Valley from Ireland. On the café's front window was a picture of bacon and eggs that looked like it had been painted by primitive man. Actually, I think Mrs. Daugherty had painted the plate of food about 30 years before. It was a frequent point of discussion around Spring Valley that the brown bacon and yellow eggs were probably the most sickly and unappetizing thing anyone had ever seen.

The Shamrock's floors were dark wood, and the walls were painted hospital white. The entire place was dotted with green photographs of Ireland and small posters with the usual American café humor: *Unattended children will be sold as slaves* and so on.

My favorite photo was of a young Tom Daugherty standing at the tail end of an English bomber. He was wearing a leather flight jacket buttoned to the neck and was smiling confidently. He had made more than a dozen flights over Germany during the war. All the flights were in the belly of that bomber, nothing but thin metal between him and the sky.

I walked back and forth fifty or sixty times before getting up the nerve to go in the café. Finally I took a deep breath, opened my coat to check that my T-shirt was tucked in and my zipper up, and then walked through the door. Keeping my head down, I strode to the counter and took a seat.

Jeanette was working behind the counter with Gwen Daugherty. I willed Mrs. Daugherty to not see me so that Jeanette could serve me. But of course Mrs. Daugherty strolled over. The veil of perfume that encircled her killed even the scent of Tom's cooking in the back. To say Mrs. Daugherty wore a lot of perfume would be an understatement as profound as saying Tony Burhold was a little bit better basketball player than I was. When Gwen Daugherty drove by in her Suburban, it smelled like a Chanel No. 5 factory had blown up nearby—even if her windows were rolled up.

"Hello, Andrew," Gwen said with her thick Irish accent. "We don't get you *inside* here very often." She winked at me. I blushed. Obviously I had not been as inconspicuous as I had imagined when I walked by—every day—hoping to catch a look at Jeanette.

I mumbled that I wanted a chocolate milk shake, then I looked around. There were a few people in the café. All of them seemed to be watching me.

"Tom! Andrew's here," Mrs. Daugherty called to her husband in the kitchen. Tom stuck his head, curly black hair first, through the opening in the wall.

I liked Tom. He coached my school soccer team in the spring, and thanks to his coaching influence we were much better at soccer than basketball. If we bugged him enough on road trips, he would tell us stories of the war and of life in Ireland before he came over. He'd played soccer in an Irish league before World War II, before he took shrapnel in his leg in that tail gunner's nest.

"Aye, it *is* Andrew," he said with a crooked smile on his square face. "The quality of our clientele improves every day. Mind he doesn't sneak out of here without paying, Gwen." He winked, and everyone in the café laughed, which made me even more uncomfortable. The other customers were all watching me. I knew a lot of them, but I couldn't get comfortable with them in there. I wished they'd leave.

Tom's head disappeared back into the kitchen. Then I noticed Jeanette was now standing right in front of me, wiping off the counter.

"Kinda cold out there for a milk shake," she said—the first words Jeanette had said to me in years. I nervously spun on the stool and looked out the window. Snow had started to fall.

Kinda cold. Her words echoed around in my empty mind. *Kinda cold.* Hmmm. I needed some sort of snappy response. No, it needed to be more than snappy, it had to be profoundly cool. The words I chose would shape the course of our relationship.

With that solemn understanding, I opened my mouth and became a babbling idiot. As near as I can recall, I said, "I, I, I like cold, cold."

I thought about running out of the café and burying myself in a snowdrift until spring. But of course there was no escape. So I turned slowly back toward the counter. And as I turned I saw Jeanette's beautiful green eyes looking at me. She held her gaze for a moment before going off to help Mrs. Daugherty make the shake.

Everything would be okay. She'd looked at me; she'd talked to me.

Jeanette squirted some chocolate in a cup and then whipped up the ice cream. It took her awhile, but eventually she sauntered over and gently placed the shake in front of me. Mrs. Daugherty was watching us over her pad as she wrote out the bill.

"Thanks," I said in an embarrassingly deep voice.

Jeanette snickered at me.

"I mean—I mean—I mean, thanks," I said, trying a high voice.

She glared at me. "You sure are weird."

"Whatdoyoumean?" I blurted out, way too fast.

"Nothing. Never mind."

"No, no, no. Iwannaknowwhatyoumeant." I couldn't slow down. I was on a runaway train to embarrassment.

"I meant that you're acting weird," Jeanette said. "But I don't know. I mean, we've never really talked. So I guess I don't know that you're acting that weird. You may act like this all the time."

"I'm not always this weird," I said, as slowly and as deliberately as my mouth would let me. "I'm not."

"Okay," she said, tilting her head slightly.

"But I am crazy about you." A dumb line, but for a moment Jeanette's cynical expression changed and she looked at me with what could almost be called a sweet expression. The world was a good place, and I was going to make it even better.

"And I came in today to ask if you'd—"

But then the door snapped opened, and a bolt of lightning flashed. In an instant my brave notions were burned to a crisp. It was Tony Burhold, carrying a basketball under his arm. Jeanette looked up and smiled brightly.

Of course, every girl in the place noticed Tony walk in. Jeanette shot a quick look around, maybe to size up the competition, then threw her arm up in the air to catch Tony's attention.

"Hi," she called out.

Tony nodded at her and walked over, bouncing the basketball on the hardwood floor. *Thump, thump, thump.* He slid onto the seat beside me.

"What d'ya say?" he asked Jeanette in a New York accent. She laughed nervously, but loud.

My face flared with jealousy. Tony was about as funny as farm machinery, but Jeanette was laughing like he'd just delivered the punch line to a great knock-knock joke. If anyone was funny in the room, it was me.

Tony pulled a menu from behind the napkin dispenser. He didn't say anything to me—he never had—but even dim-witted Tony quickly realized I was the center of attention. Suddenly they were both looking at me.

"Go on, Andrew," said Jeanette, not smiling anymore. "What were you going to say?"

It was like a bad dream in which you walk into class late and realize you're wearing Barney the Dinosaur pajamas.

"Andrew?" she said. But I couldn't speak.

The silence deepened until I couldn't take it any longer. I had to do it. Matt was right, it wasn't the end of the world if she said no *or* yes. I had to do it.

"Jeanette, I'd like to—I mean, I wanted to know if I could give you a ride home tonight?"

There was more awkward silence for a few seconds. Jeanette looked at Tony. He was glaring at me, narrowing his eyes as if he were looking into the sun.

Jeanette seemed to size up the situation for a second, saw a jealous Tony, and then grinned and said "okay" with just enough enthusiasm. "I get off at six-thirty."

I mumbled that I'd be back, dropped two dollars on the counter, and left. I didn't look back until I was out on the snow-covered road. A cold Tony Burhold was standing at the window, watching me from above Mrs. Daugherty's painted plate of eggs and bacon.

———

At half past six Jeanette was standing on the front step of the café. It was cold, and she was breathing out small puffs of warm air as I walked up. I could feel my heart beating in my throat.

"Where's your car, Andrew?" she asked, all business.

"I need you to close your eyes," I said. She shrugged and closed them.

From around the corner of the building I dragged my Rosewood glider. It was a long, wooden sled, as old as me, with room enough for two. There were foot-high railings all around and a heavy, metal steering bar at the front. On the side I had bolted the broken end of a Sherwood hockey stick so that if I ever lost control I could, in theory, pull back on it and drag the sled to a stop.

"No peeking," I said, then I told her to step up and I sat her in the glider. Then I put one of my dad's old parkas around her shoulders.

"I thought we could take the scenic way," I said.

She opened her eyes and took it all in for a moment. "You're going to pull me home?" she asked, making a mean face.

"Uh, no, just to the corner. It's downhill most of the way from there. The road is covered with snow—it's snowing," I said, letting a few flakes settle in my hand for emphasis. "I guess you know that, though, don't you?"

She didn't say anything, just sat there looking kind of amazed at my stupidity for what seemed like a long time as the snow fell and settled on her copper-colored hair. My newfound confidence was slipping away with every snowflake. I'd never recover from this blow to my ego. At school Jeanette would tease me in front of everyone. I could hear her already—"Hey, Andrew, where's your sled? In the shop? Ha, ha, ha!"

But I couldn't just stand there. I took a breath and began pulling her to the corner. We had about twenty minutes of light, more than enough to glide home. That's if it actually worked, and we didn't crash or break a ski or encounter any one of a number of other possible catastrophes.

Why wasn't she saying anything?

At the top I swallowed hard, scanned the descent for oncoming trucks or cars, sat myself in the front of the sled, and—since I heard nothing more from behind—leaned to the side and pushed us off. My life was over anyway.

The glider moved slowly at first, rumbling over a half-exposed patch of pavement. But then we hit powder as white as Kleenex and began an effortless glide through the new snow. Suddenly we were going fast—faster than I had planned. Snow began to sting my eyes. We passed the Thomas place and took a stomach-jarring dip in the road. I heard a shout from behind and turned around.

"You watch the road," called out Jeanette. She was laughing! I turned back too late, and we were heading off toward the ditch. I tried to correct our track, but the sled fishtailed one way, then another. Finally we left the road sideways and *poooofff!* We ended our short flight in a snow pile left by the road plow.

Jeanette's face and hair were covered in snow. She opened her mouth, and inside was white too. All was lost. "I'm sorry," I said pathetically.

"You *should* be!" she said, wiping off her face. "Why didn't we ever do this before?" She pulled at my coat neck and dumped a handful of snow down my back.

"Now," she said, getting to her feet and brushing off, "I bet we can get another run in before dark. This time, keep your eyes on the road." She started pulling the sled up the hill. "If you keep to the middle and quit sight-seeing, I bet our weight will carry us all the way to my house."

Jeanette pushed us off this time, and the slide on the snow-covered road took our breath in white clouds from our mouths. We slid down the hill, racing faster and faster into the coming night.

— Chapter 3 —

The Iceman

I walked Jeanette to her door after our sledding. It was cold and still snowing, but I was sweating from dragging the heavy sled.

"Thanks," I said. "I mean for letting me bring you home." We'd reached her porch, and she stood on the top step, looking down from five feet above.

"You're actually quite a creative guy, Andrew," she said.

"Nah." I leaned back on my heels and did an "Aw shucks" thing with my shoulders. "Um, you think you might want to go out sometime? Nothing serious. Just for fun."

She considered briefly. "Yeah, okay."

"How about Saturday?" I quickly suggested.

"*This* Saturday?"

"Right."

"I don't know. I guess. But only if you plan something *really* interesting for us to do."

She ran down the stairs, squeezed my arm, then ran back up and slipped inside the house. "See ya," she said as the door closed.

"Yeah," I managed to spit out while looking wide-eyed at my freshly squeezed arm.

I ran down her drive and turned for home, the heavy sled bouncing behind me. I actually caught myself humming. I was in heaven, I was—

I was finished!

The lights of our house were just in view when I stopped, forgetting that the sled would hit the back of my ankles with a hard thump.

She had told me to plan something *really* interesting for us to do. No, she had *commanded*. And by the weekend!

I walked the rest of the way home and then threw the sled in the garage. I had to find Matt. Maybe he'd have an idea.

The TV was on downstairs, and Matt was lying on the couch hidden under his red quilt. Brian Kozlowski, one of Matt's best friends, was leaning back in Dad's favorite easy chair. Matt sat up when I came down, and then he laughed at the terror in my eyes.

"Sledding didn't go over too well, huh?" he asked.

Brian looked at Matt like he wanted him to fill in the details.

"He took Jeanette McCaffrey sledding," said Matt.

"Hey-y-y!" Brian said, nodding his head respectfully.

"She thought it was fun," I added.

"Yeah, sure looks like it," said Matt.

"She did, you jerk," I said. "But maybe it wasn't such a good idea."

"Why? You lose her in a snow pile?" Brian said.

"Shut up for a minute, will you guys? She liked the sledding. But now . . . now she thinks I'm *creative*."

They laughed.

"Listen, this is serious. She wants me to take her out on the weekend, and she said that I *had* to think up something really unusual and . . . I don't know, exciting, or we can't go out. What'm I gonna do?" I whined, flopping onto our aging brown love seat.

Matt pushed the mute button on the TV remote. He thought for a second. "What's playing at the show house?" he said.

"Yeah," Brian added, "tell her you couldn't come up with anything exciting. This *is* Spring Valley, you know. There ain't *that* much to do around here."

"She could go with Tony Burhold to a movie," I answered, jumping back up and pacing back and forth in front of the glowing TV. "Tony doesn't have to be creative. And neither does Jeanette. *I* have to be creative. People like us have to be creative to get dates."

"Don't drag us into this," said Matt.

"*I* don't have to be creative," said Brian.

We heard Mom's footsteps coming down the stairs.

"Don't tell her," I whispered to Matt.

"Why?"

Mom's senses were finely tuned to pick up whispering. She stopped at the foot of the stairs and wrinkled her eyebrows together. "What are you three hiding from me?" she asked, folding her arms to show us she meant business.

"Nothing," I said.

"Jeanette McCaffrey thinks he's creative," said Matt. I kicked him.

"Seriously, what were you whispering about?" she asked, uncrossing her arms and putting her hands on her hips in her even more earnest stance.

"Serious!" Matt said, still cracking up over my pending doom. "He can't take her to a movie like a normal guy. He has to be *creative*."

"That's what she said," I added, nodding my head.

———

"She's a lovely girl," my mother said that Saturday evening in the kitchen. Fuzzy country music was coming from the radio on top of the refrigerator. I was pulling my coat on.

"Don't you try anything funny with her," she added, looking up from her magazine. My first date, and my mother already suspected me of being Attila the Hun ready to spring on our neighbor's unsuspecting daughter.

She saw my look of disgust.

"You know what I mean. Now, come here." She leaned forward in her chair. "Your first date," she said, straightening my jacket collar.

"It's not a date," I said. "We're just going to a class, that's all."

"Wait a minute! You need to drive to the college, don't you? I didn't think about that. I don't want you driving all that way at night. Let me get my purse. I'll drive you."

"I'm not going on a date with my mother!"

"Hmmm? You just said it wasn't a date."

"Okay, it's a date. Anyway, I've driven in the dark before. It's dark every morning when we go to school."

"Dark is different at night. It's darker."

"Yeah, right."

"Don't argue with me. Mothers are always right."

"Right, but irrational," I said, slipping out the back door into the cold night.

Mom's country music followed me to her pickup truck.

Yes, I thought, *it is a date. My first real date.*

I'd called Jeanette a few days after our sledding adventure. The call in and of itself was an adventure. I would dial three numbers and then hang up. Then I'd dial four numbers and hang up. It took me about an hour to finally dial all seven digits, only to discover that I was calling the Gas-'n'-Go.

When I finally did get in touch with Jeanette, everything went okay. I quickly told her that I had Saturday planned and what we'd do was a surprise. Jeanette said "sure." And while I couldn't see her face, I convinced myself that she sounded enthusiastic.

But before I turned the key in the ignition, I paused. A shiver of self-doubt ran down my spine as I thought about the challenge that I'd set for myself after I hung up that phone. I knew I had to win the heart of Jeanette Mc-Caffrey quickly, probably before the end of basketball season, only about a month away. Yes, I realized she was better looking and smarter than I was and probably only using me to make Tony Burhold jealous, but somehow I knew I could make her love me.

"She likes you," I said aloud to myself. "She *likes* you."

I fired up the truck, and within a few minutes the headlights were illuminating Jeanette's driveway and massive redwood porch. I sat in the cab for a while, hoping she would come down to the truck—so I wouldn't have to go in and meet the parents. But no such luck. Eventually I got out and climbed up onto the porch.

I rang the doorbell and waited. Inside I could hear faint scratching and bumping noises, as if Jeanette and her family were all running to find good hiding places. Then without warning a series of blinding porch lights flashed on. They weren't simple lightbulbs but a row of billion-watt spotlights that caught me like a deer in headlights.

I was still blinking from the effect when Sister Mc-Caffrey opened the door. She shot me a look of surprise, as if she expected to see the slightly taller, much better-looking figure of Tony Burhold in the door frame.

"Oh, Andrew," she said. "You must be here for Jeanette?" It was more of a question than a statement. Maybe she hoped I'd come to shovel their driveway for a few bucks.

"Yes ma'am," I answered, trying to exude confidence.

The warmth of the living room filtered out to me, but Sister McCaffrey didn't move to let me in. She was probably still thinking about this situation: Andrew Stenson was here to date her brilliant, beautiful daughter. A few of Jeanette's younger, red-haired brothers and sisters then popped into the open doorway like cherries and lemons appearing in a slot machine. They peered up at me, and I counted four small faces. I knew there were seven kids altogether.

"Oh! Come in, Andrew," Sister McCaffrey finally said, making herself turn away from my well-lit face. "I'll call Jenny."

Brother McCaffrey got up when he saw me. He let out a meager, reluctant smile, and we shook hands above the peering, small faces of Jeanette's siblings. "Evening, Andrew," was all he said to me. Then he sat back down in front of a huge TV and brought the sports page up in front of his face.

The TV droned on, throwing off flickering light that lit up the room like faraway lightning at night. But I wanted to make contact with the family, especially Brother McCaffrey.

"The Sonics lost last night," I said to his sports page. The Seattle SuperSonics were probably our closest pro basketball team. Most of the guys at school followed them.

The paper lowered, and he nodded slowly at me. "I'm not much of a Sonics fan," he said in a low voice. "I don't know why, but I've always followed the Suns, when I can get them on the satellite." He pointed his thumb toward the back wall.

I nodded thoughtfully as he brought the sports page back up. Then he peeked over and added, "Your school team's been doing all right lately, hasn't it?"

"Yeah, pretty good, I guess," I said without much enthusiasm.

"Hi, Andrew."

Jeanette was coming down the stairs like Cinderella. She was wearing light-blue jeans and a black jean jacket that looked almost new. Her hair was pulled back and left wispy in the front. The fact that she was getting dressed up for me made her look even better than usual. My mind raced for a compliment that she would like and that wouldn't make her father and her siblings look at me.

"You look, um . . . radiant," I spat out.

The paper lowered, and Brother McCaffrey chuckled. The kids laughed even though they probably didn't know what *radiant* meant.

"Thanks," she said, touching her hair.

"Be home by eleven," said her mother as we walked out.

"I think mothers have to say that or they lose their parenting license," I said to Jeanette as we climbed down the porch steps and started along her snow-covered driveway.

She stuck her hands in her pockets. "Well, if you were a parent, what would you say as your kid walked out the door?"

"Bring me back some chocolate."

She laughed. "You're weird, but you'd make a good parent."

"Thanks."

———

We were halfway to the college before I was able to think of something to break the awkward silence. "Wonder why they call it Spring Valley." I said.

"You really don't know?" she asked.

"No, I guess not."

"You've lived here all your life, and you don't know?"

"Actually we moved here when I was three."

"Hmmm," she said, not impressed. Then she said, "Well, at the east end of the valley there's an aquifer that feeds a spring that feeds a creek that feeds the Missouri. It's a very important spring, when you think about it."

"Oh. Ha. I always thought it was 'cause it was discovered in the spring, by an explorer or someone."

"No, I don't think that's right," she said. Then she reconsidered. "In fact, that seems pretty stupid."

"Yeah, I guess. Sorry."

Another "hmmm."

"What do you think your Indian name would have been?" I asked.

"You're the creative one, you give me an Indian name," she said, allowing me to redeem myself.

I swallowed. I'd gotten myself into another situation.

"Um, how about Pocahontas?"

"Uh-uh. Try again. I thought you were creative!"

I was silent for a full minute—an awfully long minute—as my mind raced. I looked out the window at the frozen fields passing by. *Wheat Woman?* No! *Pretty Woman?* No, no, no! A quick glance over at Jeanette showed she was not impressed by my hesitation and lack of instant creativity. She was starting to look at her fingernails and roll her eyes. So I spit out the next thing that came into view out the window.

"Snow!"

"Snow?" she asked slowly.

"No. Sleds with Snow in Her Mouth," I proclaimed, then looked at her again for approval of some sort.

"Not bad," she said, nodding. Then she reached over and squeezed my arm again. My nervous reaction just about sent us into the ditch.

"Oops, sorry," she said.

"No, that's okay, really. Really!"

I slowly relaxed in the glow of my most recent creative success. But then I remembered where I was taking us. It was Matt's idea. And it was bound to bomb.

———

The community college sat on the south end of Spring Valley. It was in a big, red-brick building across from a Chevron station. As we walked up to the front doors, I could hear the *ding ding* behind me as cars drove in to get a tank full of premium unleaded. Somehow that was a comforting sound. But I was walking away from it, into uncertainty.

"Still won't tell me where we're going?" Jeanette asked, grabbing my arm and holding on.

"No."

"I bet there's a dance here."

"No."

"I give up. Tell me."

I couldn't resist. "Okay. We're going to take a class."

"A class!" she said, wrinkling her nose and slumping her shoulders. She stopped on the first step into the building and grabbed onto the handrail as if she were ready to put up a good fight if I tried to pull her inside. "What kind of class? I'm smart enough already, and I get enough classes during the week. I wanted to do something fun."

"But . . . but I think you'll have *fun* in this class," I pleaded.

"I doubt it."

"Give it a try. Okay?"

She let out a big sigh.

"Please," I begged.

"Ten minutes. I'll give it ten minutes," she said, releasing her grip on the rail.

"All right!" I began breathing again, and we climbed up the stairs and followed the signs for the class down a long hall to the back door. A dozen soft lights lit up the snow-covered back parking lot, where a group of cold people were huddled around a few tables. I checked my watch. It was seven, and the teacher had already begun his introduction. The other students considered us carefully as we stood in the doorway.

"Come out, come out," the instructor said. "We need to hurry."

"It's outside? It's freezing out here," Jeanette said, pulling her coat tight around her neck and refusing to move farther out the door.

"I guess I should have told you it'd be cold," I whispered, edging her along by her elbow. "But it has to be cold or the ice will melt."

"What ice?"

"The ice we're going to sculpt," I said, moving her to the back of the class. We stopped in front of a block of ice as large as the McCaffreys' television.

"An empty canvas," the teacher was saying. "But I promise that the ice will take shape quickly. You will leave here having created something remarkable—and lasting," he added as he lifted a Polaroid camera from his table.

"I have absolutely *no* artistic ability," Jeanette said to me. "And I'm cold. Let's go."

"Just give it a minute," I whispered. I pulled off my coat and wrapped it around her shoulders.

"Large chunks of ice can be removed by using the heavy hammer and the large chisel," the instructor said. He lifted up the objects so we could identify ours.

"How about large chunks of your date's head?" said Jeanette, glaring at the hammer and then at me. I grinned back.

"Smaller shards can be chipped off with the small chisels and ice picks to your right," he continued. Again he held up the tools. "We'll all try the same design: an angel. Is everyone ready?"

"No," grumbled Jeanette, looking at the chunk of ice with fresh hatred.

"Then let's begin by removing the four corners. Place the chisel at the edge and begin tapping gently."

I handed Jeanette the hammer. She took it reluctantly. Then I bravely held the chisel in place and nodded for her to hit it. Perhaps the thought of my risking my hand for her happiness cheered her up a bit.

"Don't move," she said, taking aim. Her tongue was sticking out the side of her mouth.

Whack! Crack! A hunk of ice as big as a cantaloupe broke off and dropped heavily onto the table.

"Nice shot," I said.

"Thanks," said Jeanette.

"Excellent," said the teacher as he walked past our table. "A team effort."

Jeanette looked at me and smiled. "All right," she said. "Get that chisel in place, assistant."

I obeyed.

She was a good shot. She missed only once in the

dozen or so shots it took to remove the corners. And that throbbing thumb was worth it.

Then we both went to work with smaller chisels, half-listening to the instructor's monologue of sculpting hints. An hour and then two passed. Jeanette had given me my coat back. Eventually an angel emerged. Actually it looked more like a hunched-over football player with a bulky triangle on his back, but at least we didn't break off his wings like a lot of students did.

"Not bad, boss," I said, standing back to look at our work.

Jeanette took a bow. "I suppose you helped," she said, smiling.

A flash went off, and the sculpting teacher handed us the developing Polaroid.

"Can we have two?" I asked.

Another flash.

We drove home talking and laughing about the sculpting. Every now and then Jeanette made me turn on the overhead cab light so she could look at her picture of our hideously disfigured football player. I had just turned off the light for the fourth or fifth time when she said it.

"You know, that was the most fun I've ever had on a date."

"I didn't know if you'd enjoy it," I admitted.

"You just have to try. I'll come around." She slowly reached over and touched my arm again. This time I didn't flinch.

"How about next weekend?" I asked.

"What?"

"You want to go out again?"

She thought for a few seconds, then she said, "I guess, if you can think up something even *more* interesting for us to do."

"Uh, sure."

"Most guys just want to take me to a movie. You're so creative!" She took her hand back, but I didn't relax.

"Thanks, I think," I said. But that was all I could think to say. I had only a week to come up with the second creative date of my life. And to make matters worse, this date had to be even more interesting than ice sculpting or Jeanette would never agree to be my girlfriend. My mind was as empty as the road ahead of us.

— CHAPTER 4 —

The Burholds

Leona and Paul Burhold, Tony's parents, didn't look wrinkly and potato-shaped like most parents. Leona was thin and neat, and looked as if she should have been a real-estate agent wearing a big-shouldered, yellow jacket. Paul was tall with a wide, flat stomach and shoulders the size of basketballs. His slick brown hair was iron gray around the temples. He could have been a dentist— cool, confident. "Open wide."

But Leona did not sell houses, and Paul did not pull teeth. In fact, no one had any idea what they did for a living.

Since they attended our ward, most of us felt like we had to be nice to them. But still, no one wasted any time in asking personal questions. And for a long time we never got any answers.

"Things sure are busy down at the station," my dad had said to Paul Burhold at a ward social, just a few weeks before.

"I know what you mean," answered Paul.

"You busy?" asked my dad.

"Always."

"What exactly is it you're busy doing?"

"This and that. More this than that, though," said Paul, laughing.

Dad laughed back to be polite, and then he asked, "Do you work out of your home?" Dad was getting specific, doing his detective work. No one had ever tried to push the Burholds before, and a small crowd gathered to hear how it would turn out.

"Oh, sure, I do a little work at home, sometimes. Who doesn't?" answered Paul.

"Yeah, sure," said Dad, starting to get frustrated. "Let's try it this way. Say I wanted to buy a product or service you or your company offered. What would I get for my money?"

"Quite a lot, if I had my way about it," said Paul, slapping my dad on the back. "You come see me if you're in the market. I'll set you up." Then Paul abruptly stopped talking, as if the phone had rung, and walked off to join another small group of minglers.

———

Of course, I had been suspicious of the Burholds from the day they drove their audacious gold Mercedes into town. But, to be honest, mostly I wanted to find out what they were doing so I could get something on Tony.

And then the Dunmors' barn burned down.

Matt and I heard the sirens before we noticed the thick, black plume of smoke rising from the west. Since it was a Sunday afternoon and we had nothing better to do, we jumped in his Duster and raced toward the fire. By the time we arrived, Paul Burhold and the rest of the volunteer fire department were pulling on their yellow-and-black slickers and preparing to battle the vicious blaze eating Tiny Dunmor's barn from the inside. Tiny and his wife, Teresa, were standing by the fire truck waving their arms and screaming for the fire department to get moving, which only made the volunteers more nervous and clumsy.

Suddenly the tin roof began to make a series of loud, popping sounds, then a section curled back and flames began shooting out the top. That made Tiny and Teresa even more excited, and they began to point and run up and down the row of dressing firemen. Teresa even whacked a couple of them on the backs of their helmets.

Finally Paul Burhold grabbed a hose and ran to the side of the barn. Then Principal Walker spun a wheel on the truck, and there was water. We all cheered.

After, while Teresa was thanking the firefighters and apologizing for smacking them, Paul took Tiny's arm and walked him to the far edge of the barn. I thought he'd probably be trying to give him words of comfort, but instead Paul seemed to be asking questions and taking notes in a little blue notebook he pulled out of his shirt pocket. I wandered closer, stepping over smoldering two-by-fours, but I could hear only snippets of Tiny's answers. The only thing I heard for sure was Paul asking, "How did it make you feel?"

I inched a little closer and could almost hear them when their voices began to be drowned out by crescendo-ing laughter.

It quickly became obvious that everyone was laughing at me.

I hated that.

I looked down and realized I was standing in a pile of black charcoal and the soles of my running shoes were smoking. "Arrrgh!" I jumped away from the pile and sprinted to a snowbank near the ditch bank. I stuck the shoes in and rubbed until they were wet and cold. And ruined.

"Great."

Matt walked over, still laughing and shaking his head.

"You know, there are things in this world that the rest of us just take for granted. Like fire. We all know it's hot, but you seem—"

"Shuddup."

I looked over at Paul and Tiny. Paul had stuffed his notebook back into his shirt pocket. They were both looking at me in disbelief. Tiny was actually smiling.

I walked back to the car muttering that I wasn't finished. I would find out what the Burholds were up to.

— Chapter 5 —

Spring Valley's Most Wanted

I walked Jeanette to her door after our ice-sculpting date. She didn't kiss me, and I was too scared to try to kiss her, imagining she would scream and the blinding McCaffrey floodlights would snap on. But she did reach out and touch my arm again, which I assumed was how she showed affection.

"Thanks," she said, giving my arm a squeeze. "I can't wait for next weekend."

"I hope you had a good time," I said.

"I bet I'd always have a good time with you, Andrew," she said, and disappeared into the house.

If she hadn't said that, if she hadn't given me the hope that I was winning her over, I really believe I may not have started lying. It wasn't really as if I'd never told a lie before, but all of a sudden I was about to tell a whole bunch of lies.

"We *have* to, for school," I whined to my dad, sounding much like his police-car siren.

"We're doing this thing on law in social studies. Jeanette and I could get a really good grade if we rode around in your patrol car with you," I lied.

"I've been a cop a long time, and no other kids have ever *wanted* to ride around with me, especially for a grade," he said suspiciously. Dad was always suspicious of my motives, this time with good reason.

"Fine, I'll just fail," I said.

"Okay," he said cheerfully.

"Okay, we can come?"

"No, I'm giving you permission to fail."

"Da-a-ad."

"All right, I'll put a call in to headquarters, find out if it's okay."

"Thanks, Dad. For Saturday night, right?"

"No promises."

Matt drove the two of us to school in his old Plymouth Duster. I didn't want him to find out about the ride in Dad's patrol car. I felt guilty enough. I knew Dad would have never let Jeanette and me come along if he knew it was just for a joyride. But I couldn't think of a more exciting date.

Still, in my head *Jesus wants me for a sunbeam* was playing over and over, and with each verse I felt more ashamed of my lie.

"I'm gonna make you walk if you don't say anything," Matt said.

"I'd like to see you try kicking me out," I answered, leaning over and flexing my arm in front of his face.

"I've crushed little insects like you under my feet—without even knowing it," he said as he pushed my arm back. "You onto speaking parts yet in drama?"

Matt had convinced me to take an acting class from Mr. Larson. I usually took art, but our art teacher was out on leave having a baby. Actually, from the size of her stomach when she left, I figured she was having a living-room couch and matching recliner. So I had to choose from drama, band, or a foreign language. Of the three, acting sounded the easiest.

It *was* easy, but boring. So far we had not done any real acting. I had suffered through two months of early-morning voice training: *feeeee, fooooo, fuuuuuu* and so on. Finally we had moved on to silent acting, as Mr. Larson called it. Really it was mime. And I learned to hate mime.

"No. I don't think Larson will ever let us talk," I said. "But if you're having a party and need someone to pretend like they're riding on a train or trapped in a box, I'm your guy."

"That could come in real handy," said Matt.

"Yeah."

Mr. Larson was as skinny as Matt and I and always wore thick, brown corduroy pants and tweed jackets.

Mr. Larson grew up on a farm south of Helena and got his teaching certificate at the college in Great Falls. As far as we knew, he had never left the state of Montana in his life. So I have no idea where he picked up the English accent he affected.

But every weekday morning, first period, we got the voice.

"Ladies and gentlemen," he would say, as proper as if he were anchoring a British TV newscast. "Shall we begin?"

We would all groan and slowly pick ourselves out of our seats for the routine stretching and voice exercises and, lately, silent acting.

Mr. Larson wrote both plays the Spring Valley High School players put on every year. The first was a Christmas show about teenagers who befriend some old folks, though all the parts were usually played by teenagers, so it got kind of confusing to remember who was supposed to be old. I only went to it the year Matt had a role, and he stole the show. He played an old guy who made wise-cracks at the kids. It was closing night, and at one point he started improvising. When he pretended to stick his cane in some obnoxious kid's ear, he just about brought the house down. He was so good I forgot it was him.

The second Mr. Larson play was a silly slapstick comedy set in colonial America. Matt had played a lead role in it the year before, but even then I couldn't bring myself to go. Mom and Dad went and said it was actually pretty good. I didn't believe them. Washington and Jefferson running around with silly wigs on, singing even sillier songs:

> Oh, let's start a revolution,
> for we need a constitution.
> So strike up the band;
> we'll save this great big land . . .

Not for me, thanks.

———

Matt swung into the school parking lot. It was still early, and a light mist hung around the warm edges of the school.

I had thought about calling Jeanette the night before and offering her a ride, but I knew she rode to school on the bus, controlling her six-pack of brothers and sisters. I assumed she was there to keep them from getting off at the wrong place or something like that. And with that thought in mind, I started to pull myself out of the car into the cold morning when I saw them.

They were hard to focus on in the mist, but the two figures were unmistakable. One was small and shapely, the other tall like a bear standing on its back legs.

I squinted, and they slowly became clear. Tony had parked illegally by the side door of the school, and Jeanette was leaning up against his parents' Mercedes, giggling and twirling her gorgeous red hair. Tony was standing so close he could have reached over and twirled some hair too.

I nodded in the direction of Tony's vehicle. "Let's head in the side door," I demanded of Matt, as if I was leading a SWAT team.

"Let's not," said Matt.

"No, seriously. Come on."

"You think I'm kidding? I would not recommend walking by them," he said, then pulled his lunch bag out of the backseat. That made me momentarily forget about Jeanette.

"Geez, don't bring *that* in. You look like a dweeb," I said. "Why can't you buy your lunch like every other normal person in the world?"

Matt put the lunch bag in his teeth and locked his door.

"Anyway, why shouldn't we walk by 'em?" I asked.

He leaned back on his heels and looked into the sky. Then he breathed out a huge cloud of warm air and began. "'Cause you'll either make a fool of yourself or Tony will beat you up. Either way I'll have to try to defend you, and that will get me involved, and I don't want to get involved. Because a couple of days from now, when I've forgotten about all this, Tony will catch me in the bathroom and stick my head in a toilet, and I don't have a comb so my hair will look stupid all day and then—"

"Okay! I didn't ask for a speech. We'll go in the front door. Geez."

"It's best this way," he said.

I stuffed my hands into my jean jacket. "Tony's probably asking her out right now," I said as we crunched over the parking lot snow. "He's getting back at me for taking her home the other day. He probably wants her to come to our next stupid basketball game. So he can show off."

"The fool," said Matt. "Doesn't he know he can't compete with you—you can pretend you're trapped in a box! What could he be thinking?"

"Shuddup."

I waited by Jeanette's locker, staring up the hall toward the side door. The first bell rang, but still no Jeanette, no Tony. I was going to be late, but something wouldn't let me leave until I had seen her. Let her see my face, remember *I* was the one who had the great date ideas. I was the guy who made her laugh.

Finally they appeared in the doorway. Jeanette was unbuttoning her black jean jacket while Tony carried her books. They made their way slowly down the crowded hallway toward her locker. Jeanette was doing most of the talking, throwing her hands around.

"Hey, Jeanette!" I called out, but they were still too far away to hear exactly what I was saying. They looked up, saw me, and went back to their discussion.

Their feet were shuffling along, but it didn't seem like they were getting much closer to me. I just stood there without even a single book to hide behind, feeling more awkward with every lingering step they took. Then, just before they finally reached me, they stopped at Tony's locker. They couldn't do that! Now I had to walk over to her—onto Tony's turf.

"Morning," I said to her back.

Jeanette finished her sentence to Tony with, "I can't believe she was wearing *that*," then turned partway around. "Yeah, hi, Andrew," she said quickly.

"Who ya talking about?" I asked.

"Lisa," she said matter-of-factly.

Lisa was her best friend.

Tony looked briefly at me over the top of Jeanette's head. Then his long fingers began twirling the combination of his locker.

"I think I have Saturday night all set," I said to Jeanette.

"Oh, fine."

Then, before I could get my next sentence out, Tony broke in. "Get a load of this, Jenny," he said, pulling a magazine out of his locker.

Jeanette moved close to Tony and his basketball magazine and then—then she grabbed his arm! I gasped and moved closer, pretending to be interested in the magazine, but Tony rolled it up. So there we were, the three of us standing so close we could have been dancing, and Tony and Jeanette were carrying on a conversation like I wasn't there. I felt incredibly awkward, but I wasn't about to leave her alone with him until she let go of his arm.

Eventually she did, and I stepped back into the now-empty hallway. I was late, and I had to get to class. So I left them alone and began walking down the hall. I had taken only about three steps when I heard Jeanette say, "You don't have to leave, Andrew. I'll talk to you."

I was sure she didn't mean any offense by that sentence, but it sliced through my skin and tore a chunk out of my heart. *I'll talk to you.* Like I needed her to talk to me! Well, I did, but that wasn't the point.

"I'd better get to class," I mumbled without turning around, then jogged to drama.

———

"Just take it easy," Matt told me on the drive home. "You're not serious with Jeanette. It doesn't matter if she talks to another guy."

"This isn't just any other guy," I told him. "This is Tony Burhold. Why does it have to be him? She squeezed his arm. And did I tell you he called her Jenny! Her mom calls her Jenny. I've never called her Jenny. I've never heard anyone else call her Jenny."

"You *did* have to pick one of the best-looking girls in school," Matt said. "You expect the rest of the male population to ignore Jenny from now on?"

"It's Jeanette to you, loser. And yes, I expect them to ignore her."

We pulled onto our road and started the descent down the hill. I sighed at Jeanette's house as we passed.

"You gonna take her out again this weekend?" Matt asked.

"Yeah. I'll probably call her tonight. Dad's taking us in the patrol car on Saturday night." Oops. I hadn't meant to tell him about that.

"Hmmm?"

"What?"

"Nothing."

Dad had let Matt and me come along on patrol a couple of times before. But we had never been allowed to bring anyone else. We'd never really argued about that rule. Usually patrolling was boring: just sitting on the highway watching cars, or cruising up and down the ten-mile stretch between Spring Valley and the turnoff to Great Falls. That was Dad's territory. But maybe Jeanette would think it was fun. After all, pulling over speeders on the highway gave you a rush, for a few seconds anyway.

"You sure are growing," Elna said to me.

Jeanette and I were sitting on the wooden bench just outside Elna's dispatch office. Jeanette kind of snorted at Elna's compliment. She covered her mouth with her hands to contain herself.

"Thanks, Elna," I said, checking my watch and then staring at the wanted posters plastered all over the bulletin board. "You hear from my dad yet?"

"Just relax. He'll be along soon. He usually swings by about seven, his break time." She laughed as if she'd told a joke, and we looked at each other, not really sure why she was laughing or if we should laugh along.

At about ten after seven—and after my seventeenth check of the time—the lights of Dad's patrol car filled the station house window. I stood up and watched as Dad slowly pulled himself out of the car. He walked around the vehicle, kicking the tires. Then he reached inside the car again, popped the hood, and began to check the oil. It finally struck me that he was doing this to bug me, so I rapped on the window and shook my fist at him.

Eventually he made it inside. "Hi, Jeanette," he said. He opened up his parka and hung his hat by the door.

"Hi, Brother Stenson," she said lightly. "Thanks for letting me ride with you. This should be fun."

All I could do was hope she didn't say anything to give away the fact that this was a date and not a school assignment.

"Just got a little paperwork, kids. Won't take me five minutes," he said. "Andy, get me a drink, will you?" He handed me some change, and I headed for the pop machine. All of a sudden I was part of the highway patrol team. I felt important.

Dad and Elna filled out whatever forms they needed to, and we were on our way. Jeanette and I rode in the back behind a screen. Dad was hidden by the hood of his big parka.

"Once around the park, driver," I said as Dad pulled out of the station-house lot. He looked back at me around the parka's puffy hood with his eyebrows raised—his *don't push it* eyebrow thing.

Without saying much of anything, Dad had a way of convincing you to shut up, or get up, or do something, or stop doing something. I suppose that's what made him so good at his job. He wasn't a big guy, not even average height or build, really. But he had a way of acting big that made him seem several inches taller and about fifty pounds heavier than he was.

And I think he had the whole town fooled.

I noticed it in subtle ways. Once, before a ward social, someone wanted to move the piano outside onto the lawn. "Get Russ," said one of the ladies. "He'll lift it by himself." Yet when the men did lift the piano, I was probably the only one who noticed that Dad had to lift his corner up to his chest just to keep it even with the other guys' waists.

"You ain't so big," I told him once a few years before. I was mad, and we were arguing about something I was supposed to do but didn't. I instantly regretted saying it, but I couldn't stop myself.

"I'm bigger than you," he said. And that was true at the time.

"Yeah, but you always act so tough. You try to scare me and Matt into doing stuff. That's not fair."

He pondered that for a minute. It even made him stop being angry and sit down, rubbing his chin with his hand.

"You're probably right," he said quietly. "Intimidating people is just part of my job, I suppose." He looked up at me. "Well, if I can't intimidate you into doing your chores around here, how do you propose I motivate you?"

Tough question. It left me speechless.

"Okay, when you think of a better way, let me know."

During the next few years, I must have thought of a hundred better ways for him to get us to do our chores, but I never had the nerve to tell Dad. It wasn't because I was afraid of him; he never hit us or anything. But it slowly sunk in that I really didn't want him to lose the ability to appear bigger than he was. I felt better about him keeping that skill sharp for when he pulled over speeding maniacs on the freeway.

And hey, we were just about to pull one of those maniacs over now. Dad was edging onto the freeway when a black Mazda with tinted windows passed us at the speed of sound. Dad hit the siren and lights, and we took off. Jeanette grabbed my right hand, and I held onto the door with my left.

Dad picked up the radio. "Elna, I'm following a guy in a black sports car—"

"Mazda Miata," Jeanette and I said in unison, then looked at each other and laughed. The adrenaline was rushing already.

"A black Mazda Miata, my backseat drivers tell me. I clocked him at eighty-five," he said, turning the radar so we could see it. We both said "hmmm" in appreciation.

"Seems he doesn't want to stop and chat," said Dad as the black car accelerated.

Dad floored the patrol car, and within a minute we'd caught up to him, our speedometer flickering near a hundred. He was now in our headlights. "Can you two make out that license? I can't."

"8-1-3-V-L-T," said Jeanette proudly. I knew Dad could read the license; his eyes were great. He was just including us in the excitement.

"Elna, we've got some young eyes in the chase tonight. You get that number? It's a Washington plate."

"Sure did. I'll call it in," Elna crackled.

"Still doesn't want to slow," said Dad. "Probably late for a haircut. Elna, you'd better get the boys in Great Falls out on the road, just in case our test pilot here decides to keep going on to Canada."

"Already called them," Elna crackled to us.

"I'll give you a pay raise tomorrow," said Dad.

"That'll be the day," said Elna, and we could hear her laughing again.

We'd slowed to ninety or so by then, keeping the black Mazda just in the far limit of our high beams. We flew toward Great Falls on dry roads, passing no other vehicles.

Soon we saw the red, yellow, and blue reflection of highway patrol lights in the distance. Within a minute we had lights in front, behind, and on the side of us.

The Mazda slowed to about sixty, sped up again as if rethinking the decision, and then eventually pulled over to the highway shoulder and stopped. The Great Falls cops jumped out and surrounded the Mazda.

"Stay here," said Dad, looking back at us.

"Be careful," said Jeanette.

"Yeah," I added.

Dad slammed the door shut, and we watched as he and four Great Falls officers approached the Mazda with their guns drawn. The driver got out, and Dad spun him around and cuffed him.

"Cool," I whispered. I couldn't have asked for a better night to take Jeanette out.

I reached around the seat and rolled down Dad's window a few turns so we could hear what was going on.

"He's yours," one of the Great Falls guys was saying. "We don't want him."

"Like I want the work," Dad said back. "The only reason he stopped is because of you boys. You fellas deserve the recognition."

Finally Dad came back to the patrol car and had Elna call Irwin Gork's tow truck for the Mazda.

"I could drive the Miata," I told Dad.

"Yeah," Dad said, pulling out a pad of forms. "Then when you wreck I can pay for it until I'm ninety-five."

We got out of the back seat to make room for the speeder. Dad pushed the guy's head down so he could fit into the squad car. Then he went back to search the Mazda.

Jeanette and I got in the front seat. The next few minutes were real awkward as Jeanette and I pretended not to want to turn around. Finally I looked at the guy. He was not too old, maybe thirty, unshaven and wearing an expensive-looking leather bomber jacket. His mouth was twitching on one side.

"Probably a drug runner," I whispered to Jeanette as quietly as I could.

"What?" she said back.

"Doesn't matter," I said a little louder.

Finally Jeanette turned around. "Why didn't you stop?" she asked.

For a second the speeder ignored her. He was looking out the front window at my dad, who was using his flashlight to search the Mazda's trunk. Finally he turned to Jeanette and snarled, "You guys little cops?" Then he grunted a half-laugh.

"Russ, you there?" Elna's voice crackled over the speaker.

I picked up the radio mike. "Elna, Dad's outside. You want me to get him?"

"You'd better, Andrew," she said. "I have a little news about the car you stopped."

The guy in the back stiffened. He looked like someone had reached over and given him a wedgie.

"You mind getting my dad?" I asked Jeanette, not trusting the speeder alone with my date.

She popped out of the car and brought Dad back.

"Seems you might have a celebrity," said Elna. "The car is registered to a Mitch Reynolds."

"*The* Mitch Reynolds? The Sonic guard?" asked my dad. We all turned around to look at the guy in the back seat. No, this guy wasn't the Mitch Reynolds we'd seen on TV, hitting sky-high three pointers.

"That's what Helena tells me," Elna added. "His car went missing from his house in Seattle three days ago. I'm sure he'll be happy to get it back. Maybe he'll send us some tickets."

A bad word from the backseat.

"This is the best date I've ever been on!" said Jeanette, which was answered by raised eyebrows from my dad.

———

After leaving the highway patrol station, Jeanette and I got something to eat, and then I drove her home.

"Pretty exciting, huh?" I asked as I pulled Mom's pickup into her driveway.

"Wait till I tell Lisa about this," she said. "She'll be so-o-o jealous."

I stopped the vehicle at the end of the driveway but didn't move to get out. After a date like that, I deserved a kiss. In fact, I had to have a kiss. It was the necessary next step on my way to making Jeanette my girlfriend. Not that I was that sure of my kissing abilities, but I'd practiced on my pillow the night before. After all, how hard could it be?

Of course, I sure wasn't bold enough to just lean over and try my luck, so I sat with my hands welded to the steering wheel.

"What time is it?" Jeanette finally asked me.

I turned my watch hand slightly. "Little after eleven," I said.

"Well, I'd better be going in," she said. "If my mom sees us out here, she'll turn on the porch lights and they'll tease me all night."

I swallowed at the thought of the McCaffreys' porch lights flashing on and illuminating my guilty face. I hadn't done anything, but if her parents looked out the window I was sure they'd know I was thinking stuff.

"Okay," I said reluctantly and swung myself out of the truck cab. Jeanette waited for me to come around and open her door. She stepped out, and as she did she ran her fingers along my neck. That was all, but I remained paralyzed in place, doomed to freeze in her driveway.

"Andrew?" she called from her doorway. "You're supposed to see me to the door. Those are the rules."

"Uh, yeah, sorry," I managed to stutter before running up the porch steps to her.

"Thanks for a great night," she said.

"No problem. I'll think up something great for next weekend!"

"Can't wait," she said, leaning forward and whispering in my ear.

Oh boy, this was it. I was going to get a kiss. But just as I moved forward and puckered, Jeanette with one smooth movement backed into her house and was gone. I didn't even have a chance to react, she was so quick.

Again I'd broken new records for dating creativity. But my plan to win her over had not advanced past the blueprint. I felt so crushed I just stood on her doorstep for a full ten minutes, listening to the scurryings inside the McCaffrey house and unable to move.

— CHAPTER 6 —

A Door to Suspicion

After the incident at the Dunmors' barn, I'd kept watching the Burholds. And a few weeks later I saw them with that notebook again, this time at the retirement home.

Matt and I were there with Mom and Dad visiting Dad's Aunt Bess. Bess didn't usually recognize us, but she liked having company to talk to. But after half an hour of talk about the old days, Dad sent me down the hall to find a pop machine. He liked his pop.

I walked by an open doorway, and there they were, Paul and Leona, sitting in an old guy's room. The guy was talking to Leona while Paul took notes. I passed by nonchalantly and then glued myself to the wall and tiptoed back to the door.

"That was 1917—no, 1918," the guy was saying.

"Tell us about that storm," said Leona. "You say it isolated the town from the outside?"

"Well, back then we used to get our food trucked in from Great Falls a couple of times a week. When the roads were clogged, we'd get our supplies brought in by train," the old guy said.

"But yeah, after that storm the road from Great Falls was closed and there was six feet of snow on the lines. A week passed, and Mavis and I were down to our last egg. Well, she made a cake and set it out on the back doorstep and we were inside. We could hardly wait to dig into that cake. We let a few minutes pass, and we went out to get it, and there's the neighbor's Saint Bernard licking his lips."

Paul and Leona laughed.

"And I think everyone was down to their last cup of flour or last swig of milk when a snow cat finally broke through with supplies."

"Fantastic," said Paul. I could hear him scribbling furiously.

Why were the Burholds concerned about how they got supplies to a shut-off town in 1918? Did they think Spring Valley would be isolated again? And why had they cared about Tiny Dunmor's feelings after his barn fire? Had they set the blaze?

They weren't talking anymore.

I bit my bottom lip and peeked around the corner. Paul, Leona, and the old guy met my glance. Part of my open jean jacket must have been visible through the doorway. They obviously realized someone was snooping.

"Yes?" said Paul in his usual cool voice.

"Uh, hi. I was just looking for my Aunt Bess. She's not here."

I made a getaway from the door and whacked myself on the forehead with my palm. Another failure.

———

I knew the Burholds were up to something, but after weeks of suspicion I had nothing more on them. And more important, that meant I had nothing on Tony.

— CHAPTER 7 —

Creative Heights

I was running out of time.

During the next week it became obvious that Tony was paying much more attention to Jeanette, hanging around her at school and giving her rides home from the café.

I had to take the plan to the next level. I had to make her mine, and I needed something big. And that's just what I found, by luck.

I was in the school library during a free period. I started flipping through a copy of the Spring Valley newspaper for the sports when I saw the ad buried in a corner below the basketball scores.

It was perfect. Romantic and yet dangerous. It would take almost all of the money I had hidden in the ceiling of my room. But it would be worth it. Definite impressing material.

When I passed Matt's door on my way to bed that Friday night, he was reading, big stockinged feet up on his desk and leaning back in his chair. By then there were only a dozen or so hours before my first official day date with Jeanette. I stuck my head inside his room.

"First day game tomorrow," I said. Matt looked up from his magazine and wiggled his toes at me from one end to the other like little people doing the wave at a football game.

"You're sinking further into the mire of hopelessness," he said. "And you're an idiot to spend all that money. I thought you were saving to buy a car."

"Oh, I'm sorry, Dad, I thought this was Matt's room."

"All right, no lecture. Go, spend, be ignored."

"I'm not being ignored."

Matt went back to his magazine.

"Why do you think I'm being ignored?" I demanded.

"Never mind. You're not," he said.

"Tell me what you mean, or I'll come in there and slug you."

"You won't like what I've got to say, so don't make me say it."

"Now you *have* to tell me. Tell me!"

"Okay, you're acting like a lovesick moron. There, I said it. I'm sure Jeanette acts like she likes you when you're on dates out where nobody knows you. But at school and church she acts like an ice queen to you."

"What do you know?" I asked harshly. He was a jerk.

"Most girls flirt with guys they like," he continued. "They look for them in the halls, sit by them in Sunday School, call them at home. All I'm saying is, Jeanette doesn't act that way to you except when you're both around Tony Burhold."

He paused. "Aw, what do I know? Maybe she's just different than other girls."

"Yeah, what do you know?" I spat.

"The only thing is, she acts flirty and nice around Tony all the time."

I lunged into the room and pushed him and his leaning chair over. His chair crashed to the carpet, and he lay there stunned.

"Jerk," I said, and stormed out.

"You're being used!" he yelled after me.

I got to my room and flopped onto my bed. From under my pillow I pulled out the picture of Jeanette and me with our ice angel. In the photo Jeanette was smiling, holding up a hammer and chisel triumphantly. *She does look evil,* my mind told me. *She's just using me to make Tony jealous.*

The thought slipped from my brain and inched down my spine, settling in the pit of my stomach. I curled into a ball and listened to myself breathe.

"No, she will like me," I finally said.

I got up and slowly began bouncing up and down on the balls of my feet, trying to snap myself out of my misery. With each bounce I became more and more convinced that Jeanette would soon get used to the idea of loving me.

"Tomorrow," I said out loud. "I'll win her over tomorrow."

———

Picking up Jeanette in the daytime proved to be a breeze compared with the traumatic experience it was at night. When Jeanette answered the door, the porch lights did not snap on to blind me. Her numerous brothers and sisters were off playing somewhere. And even her mom and dad were nowhere to be seen. She came out the door pulling on a puffy coat over a thick sweater, which was the same color as her green eyes.

"Dressed warm?" I asked.

"Yeah, thanks for the warning this time." She pulled the door closed behind her. "We're not going ice sculpting again, are we?"

"That wouldn't be a very creative date, now would it?"

"No. And you *are* the most creative dater I know."

"Thanks," I said, blushing.

We climbed into Mom's truck, pulled out of the Mc-Caffrey driveway, and made our way to the freeway entrance. We headed toward Great Falls.

"You didn't tell me we were going out of town," she said.

"What's the matter? You'd have brushed your teeth better if you knew we were going to Great Falls?" Oops, I was too cocky.

She sneered. "No, I just wanted to get back early."

I knew why she wanted to get back. There was a dance at the gym that night. Tony would be there, of course. I had already decided that I must do whatever was necessary to keep Jeanette away from that gym.

"We'll probably be back in time," I lied, hoping she would soon be having such a good time that she would forget about the dance and Tony.

"But you have to put all unessential things out of your mind for now. We're going on an adventure."

"I love adventures," she said. "As long as I don't break a nail."

I looked over at her. I knew she could be kind of mean, but was she really vain too?

She saw my look. "That was a joke, Bozo," she said, hitting me in the shoulder.

"Oh. Oops. Ha, ha."

"No one appreciates my finely tuned sense of humor."

"I'm sure you'll get the recognition you deserve after you die. That's what happens to all the great ones."

She laughed. She was the perfect girl.

The day was warm and bright for the middle of winter. Great Falls was about an hour's drive, but I liked having Jeanette all to myself with no distractions. I asked her all the questions I could think up, and she happily answered them. After I ran out of things to ask about, we sat quietly listening to Mom's truck make the low, rhythmic rumble of a clothes dryer.

And then in no time the first Great Falls exit sign appeared.

"We take the second exit," I said with authority.

"Am I allowed to know yet what kind of adventure we're going on?" Jeanette asked.

"Oh, sure," I said. "But I'd have to kill you. It's top secret!"

"Just a hint?"

"Hasn't anyone ever told you what top secret means? It means there is absolutely *nothing* more secret. If I were a secret, and I were a *top* secret, you would not even know I existed. I would be invisible, unspeakable."

We passed the first exit.

"Are you telling me that where we're going is a secret?" Jeanette said, smiling lightly.

"You catch on real quick. No wonder you're an honor student."

Jeanette looked into one of the fields, where a couple of horses were racing along the fence line.

"We're going horseback riding?" she guessed.

"Uh, no," I said.

"That's probably good," she said. "As I recall, you have a pretty unusual riding style."

I swallowed hard, remembering the time I met Jeanette. It was April. I know the month because I had just turned ten a few days before, at the most a week before. I had come of age, Matt told me.

When I went outside that morning, Matt was sitting on the high cedar fence that kept our horses from getting to my mom's sad-looking veggie garden. Matt jumped down when he saw me and ran over. He was smiling a big, toothy grin, and without saying a word he began pushing me and pretending to box. Then he turned and raced back to the fence, so I ran after him.

Matt had one of our horses, Blaze, already saddled, and Sweet Pea was bridled and tied to the fence.

"You put her saddle on," he said. It was the first time Matt had let me saddle a horse, and my eyes widened with pride.

It was heavy, but I didn't ask for help. Sweet Pea stood patiently while I tried to push it up onto her back.

After a few tries I realized it was going to be impossible from the ground; other than the snowplow, I think Sweet Pea was the largest moving thing I'd ever seen. So I slowly climbed the fence pulling the saddle after me, and then with a surge of effort I threw it onto her. The moment the saddle hit her back, her chest blew up like a balloon.

"Wow! You see that?" I asked Matt.

He shrugged. "Just don't cinch up the saddle too tight," he said. "It might bother old Sweet Pea."

"Okay," I said, climbing down from the fence. "Thanks."

Matt began to snicker. I didn't know what was funny, so I just smiled back.

I left the cinch loose and then pulled myself up onto Sweet Pea's back. Since the saddle was loose, I had to straighten it by adjusting my weight. But then we were ready. Matt trotted Blaze out of our drive, and I followed, starting up the lane toward town. Mrs. Thomas's collies, who were at our place sniffing out a culvert for skunks, saw us leave and ran ahead at a full sprint, biting each other on the neck, excited to be going somewhere.

It was a grand Montana spring morning, and riding high on Sweet Pea's back I felt like the explorer who'd discovered Spring Valley.

I saw Jeanette from half a mile away. Her family had just moved into the yellow house with the covered porch about halfway along our road. I'd seen her in church the week before. She was probably the first girl I'd really ever noticed, though that didn't sink in at the time.

As we rode up, she was leaning on the wood rail of her front porch and waving at us. We were too cool to wave back, so we nodded.

Well, to be honest I wanted to wave, but I was too petrified of girls to do much of anything. Then again, I thought the impressive sight of me atop our black mare would set her heart to fluttering.

"Nice horses," Jeanette called out. I grinned back, gaining confidence. "Where are you going?" she asked.

"Aw, we're just riding up to the old barn," said Matt, pointing to the hill behind her place. There was a winding trail through the mature, green field that lead to Mrs. Thomas's decaying hay barn.

"Wish I knew how to ride," she said. "My mom said we might get a horse."

I was going to say something at that moment, something profound and impressive. But instead I tried to straighten my saddle some more. I shifted my weight a little just as Sweet Pea let out a great breath, and before I knew what was happening the saddle and I had slipped underneath the horse.

I was still in the saddle, but I was hanging upside down. Mrs. Thomas's collies bounded over to lick my face.

Matt was wailing with laughter. Jeanette was laughing. I was humiliated.

"Shuddup," I said. I let go and tumbled onto the ground.

"Didn't you cinch your saddle up tight?" asked Jeanette. "Everyone knows you're supposed to do that."

———

I shook off the bad memory and mumbled, "No horse-back riding," which Jeanette ignored.

———

I hadn't counted on her being able to see the hot-air balloon before we even reached the second exit. But as we rounded a bend, there was my secret in a field on the side of the freeway. The balloon was half-inflated and looked like a fifty-foot blue-and-red beanbag left by some giant.

Actually, I hated heights. I cursed myself when I saw the thing. It suddenly was real. My stomach tightened with the same feeling I got when I would be sitting comfortably on the bench during a basketball game and coach would out of the blue call me in to spell Tony.

"Are we going up in that?" Jeanette asked, wide-eyed.

"Yeah, I guess. That okay?"

"That's wonderful!" she said, grabbing the dashboard. "I've always wanted to go up in a balloon."

"No kidding?" That made me feel a little more at ease.

"Yeah." She leaned forward to get a better look. Her breath steamed up the front window. "This is great!" she said, bouncing on the truck's bench seat. "Hurry up, hurry up!"

By the time we pulled onto the field, the balloon was nearly full. Thick ropes tethered it to the earth, but I knew that once they were released there would be nothing but a flimsy wicker basket to keep us from dropping several hundred—or thousand—feet. I remembered popping Matt's birthday balloons one year, how the tied end twisted and flew about before scrunching against a wall. I looked around the sky for big pins.

"Now you're *sure* you want to do this?" I asked Jeanette, trying to act worried about her feelings instead of my own neck.

"Come on," said Jeanette, grabbing her puffy coat and jumping out of the pickup. "You chicken or something?"

"Ha, right," I answered, but she was out of the truck cab. I opened the door and stuck my head out. "I'm no chicken. It was *my* idea, you know."

"Blah, blah, blah," said Jeanette, her back to me. "Will you hurry up? They'll take off without us."

"I doubt it. We're the only passengers on this trip."

———

"I'm Lou Steele," said the pilot in one of those deep, calm voices airline pilots use to reassure their passengers that it's normal to lose a wing. He shook my hand with an iron grip. He squeezed so hard all my knuckles cracked out loud like wet firewood on a campfire. Then he shook Jeanette's hand much more gently.

"Just relax. We'll be ready to take off in about fifteen minutes," said Steele. He was a sturdily built man with an abnormally thin waist that made his thick chest seem cartoonishly large. Then I noticed his wavy, gray hair. It was probably gray from too many close calls in popped balloons.

"I'm Lou Steele," I whispered to Jeanette after our pilot had returned to his balloon. I did it in a deep voice, but Jeanette didn't laugh.

"Quit it. He looks nice," she said.

I did my best deep voice impression: "I am nice. I'm Lou Steele. Just relax, baby."

She looked at me out of the corner of her eyes—a *shut up* look.

"All aboard," yelled Steele after a long wait. We ran across the field, and he pulled us in. Then he strapped some safety lines on us, and three of his helpers slowly brought the balloon's cables together and we started to rise. I grabbed onto the side of the basket so tightly my knuckles turned white. Jeanette was right next to me, or I would have closed my eyes. I wanted to ask Steele how many of these things pop—just a rough average—or how many of his riders fall out in a normal week. But of course I couldn't ask him anything that would show I was scared. Not deep-voiced Steele.

"When the breeze is right, we can usually drift down the highway and get quite a view of the city," Steele said loudly over the rush of the propane. I nodded quickly, and he winked at me. Obviously I didn't have to ask a stupid, scared question; he knew I wasn't having fun.

"Look. There's a football field," said Jeanette. She was leaning on the side of the basket as calmly as if she was at the counter of the Shamrock taking an order. She wasn't even holding on!

"Ugh sas if," I managed to say as my stomach rolled over.

"What?" said Jeanette.

"I see it," I said, slowly.

Steele, his jacket open, oblivious to the cold, was fiddling with the valve that I assumed regulated the bursts of fire that whooshed every now and then. I hoped he was trying to give us some privacy and that the valve really didn't need such close inspection. It was getting cold—Siberian cold. I wanted to put my arm around Jeanette, but my arms were attached to my hands, and I needed both of those to hold onto the side of the basket.

Arrgh! I thought.

"I bet we could see all the way to home from up here," Jeanette said.

"Where do you kids live?" asked Steele.

"Spring Valley," answered Jeanette. We all looked into the distance, past the city. I couldn't see much that way; it was too hazy. But we all squinted for awhile.

"Nah," Steele finally said. "On a clear day, though, you have a good view of the Rockies from up here."

"How high are we?" I asked. Somehow that seemed important.

"Oh, I don't know. Not too high yet. Maybe eight hundred, a thousand feet," Steele said. "Too far to jump out, that's all I know."

I got the overwhelming thought right then that I'd like to be able to float. Then I could get out and down to the ground, out of the creaking wicker basket.

And so I logically said, "You think if they filled a guy up with helium, he could float?"

Steele and Jeanette looked at me as if I was an idiot.

I smiled the best I could.

Jeanette quickly forgot my remark and started bouncing around, making our tiny wicker perch rock back and forth. She looked over every side, pointing out the people and the cars. I just stayed on the same side, turning my head slightly to see what she wanted me to.

Eventually Jeanette made her way back to where I stood. She leaned against me and put her head on my shoulder. Then I was frozen not only by the cold and the height but by being so close to Jeanette.

"Thanks," she said. "This is incredible."

"No problem," I managed to say.

"You nervous or something?" Jeanette asked without a hint of compassion. She lifted her head and stared into my wide eyes and then laughed at me.

"No," I answered, loosening my death grip on the side of the basket. I even managed to bring up one hand to touch my hair to show how cavalier I was.

"Let's spit on someone," I said. She smiled briefly.

Then we leaned against the side and took in the city. We were drifting over the river just outside town, where the fields were clean and white. Pretty soon I imagined Jeanette and myself married and living in one of the apartment buildings we were floating over, or maybe in one of the fancy houses down by the river. One house had a large yard with manicured bushes and a tennis court. To get a house like that, Jeanette would have to be a lawyer or scientist or something, making lots of money. Me? Hmmm. I had no idea what I could do in life. I knew I'd go on a mission, but after that? Maybe I'd work in a restaurant, be a chef. I liked food.

Then I wanted to know what Jeanette was dreaming about.

"What you thinking?" I asked.

"Nothing. You wouldn't understand."

"Sure I would. Tell me."

"I was thinking about being up here with the cumulus, the clouds. From the ground they look solid, massy, like mountains. But up here you see how fragile they really are. It's a wonder they even hold together as much as they do. You read this stuff, but up here it's more real. What were you thinking?"

"Aw, you don't want to know."

"You have to tell me. I told you what I was thinking."

"I was thinking about clouds too," I joked.

"Yeah, right. Tell me, or I'll push you out." She grabbed my arm and threatened to use it to lever me out of the basket.

I had to do it. I had to try for the next level.

"All right. I was wondering if you're my girlfriend."

She dropped my arm.

"See, I told you you didn't want to know."

We drifted for a few more minutes before she spoke.

"No, we're not boyfriend and girlfriend," Jeanette said. "But I like being with you. You are the most creative guy I've ever met. And I think we've become friends."

"Just friends?" I asked.

"Yes. But that's good. Friendships often develop into more later. You agree, don't you?"

"I guess."

I looked over the edge for a pond or lake to jump into, but they were all frozen and a long, long way down. I'd spent my life savings on a girl who had just given me the old I-want-you-as-a-friend speech.

But as we floated silently over a hill where kids were sledding, I reconsidered what she had said. Maybe she was really trying to tell me that we were laying the groundwork for a much more meaningful relationship, much more meaningful than she could ever have with dangerous, witless Tony.

Just then Captain Steele's balloon started losing altitude and we were descending back toward Great Falls. I grabbed onto the side of the basket with both hands.

"That's the ride, kids. We're going to try to land in that field," Steele said to us.

"What do you mean *try* to land in that field?" I demanded. "What happens if you miss? Do you miss a lot?"

"Not too much. Don't worry, it's been pretty calm today." His gray hair swirled slightly in a cross breeze.

Ahead of us, the sun was shooting long red ribbons across the darkening sky. Well below us, Steele's helpers were getting ready for our arrival. They slowly got bigger as we dropped. I scanned the horizon for the nearest hospital. Nope, not even an official-looking building on this side of town.

"The trick is missing the power lines," said Steele. "They'll barbecue you in the blink of an eye."

Jeanette and I peered back over the side. We were a hundred feet up and just coming over a set of thick power lines. I decided I would jump out before letting them fry me. But we drifted easily over the lines, and Steele brought us down with a heavy thump onto dear old Mother Earth. I wanted to jump out and kiss the ground, but I was too queasy to move very fast.

———

We pulled into the first fast-food place we saw, a greasy-looking burger place just into Great Falls. Jeanette ordered a milk shake but seemed disappointed when it came. Somehow it wasn't what she expected. I had to admit it didn't look as good as the shakes at the Shamrock.

She was using a fork to scoop the sloppy chocolate mixture out of a Styrofoam cup. Most of it dripped back into the cup before she could slurp it up.

"I can't believe you're not hungry," she said, wiping her mouth with a napkin that was already brown and soggy. "I was starving."

"Nah. This is fine." I was clutching a cup of water like I was afraid someone might take it away. I didn't think my stomach could handle much more than water, so I held on tight.

"I remember you like chocolate shakes," she said. "But this isn't as good as the ones I make."

"No, I'm fine."

"Hey, I forgot about the dance," said Jeanette. "What time is it?"

I loosened my grip on the glass and checked my watch. "Six-thirty," I said. I wished it was a few hours later. We still had lots of time to make the dance.

"You want to head back?" she asked, pushing her seat out. Obviously it wasn't a question; she was ready to leave.

"We just got here. You got someone waiting for you at school?" I snapped. I couldn't hide my annoyance at the thought of going to the dance and having to share Jeanette. If she were my girlfriend, it would be different. But she was on the open market, and I didn't like my chances in such surroundings.

To be honest, I'd never enjoyed dances. When I asked girls to dance, too many of them said the same thing: "Oh, okay, I guess." The phrase hardly provided a shot of adrenaline to my ego.

Jeanette unhappily pulled her chair back up to the table. "Fine, we'll stay."

"I'm sorry. I just took a lot of time planning this day. I thought we could maybe take a walk downtown or something. Matt told me if you stare into the lights at city hall long enough, everything turns sort of purple. You have to stare for awhile, though."

"Okay, let's go," said Jeanette, as if she were hurrying us to catch a bus.

———

We didn't make it back in time for the dance. And at Jeanette's front door, I again came away without a kiss, which by this time wasn't really a surprise.

Obviously I needed to take a different approach. I needed to get Tony out of the picture. And that meant getting something on his parents.

— CHAPTER 8 —

Spying on the Burholds

After months of suspicion, all my theories about the Burholds came together on a Monday night at the Shamrock Café.

Dad was on patrol, so Mom, Matt, and I went out to eat.

When we ate at the Shamrock, I always ordered Tom Daugherty's famous roast beef sandwich dripping with rich, salty gravy. The roast beef was piled high on thick slabs of homemade white bread. During the first few bites, it was succulent, flavorful, brilliantly delicious.

But about halfway through the meal, Tom's salty gravy started taking over the dining experience. Suddenly the inside of your mouth was covered in gravy the thickness of used motor oil. And you became very, very thirsty. You found your tongue salty, sticky, and too heavy to move. You absolutely, positively could not continue eating.

"You didn't finish," Tom said to me once, looking down at my half-finished plate of roast beef, bread, and gravy. "Didn't you like it?" He didn't seem too upset. He actually seemed to be enjoying the fact I hadn't finished.

"It's just, well, it's a little salty," I said apologetically.

"Supposed to be that way."

"Why?"

"Let's put it this way: for a few bites it was the best roast beef sandwich you ever had. Am I right?"

"Yeah, sure. But I wanted it to be the best for more than just a couple of bites."

"No," said Tom, "can't work that way. I've found I can make a delicious roast beef sandwich or an average sandwich. The only problem is, the delicious one gets salty after a while. So I had to say to myself, 'Tom, why don't you make something memorable.'"

I had downed our entire pitcher of water before I finally got Jeanette's attention. She rolled her eyes in her usual way but did bring us more. She was putting the plastic water pitcher on our table when out of the corner of my eye I saw a large shadow pass by the diner window. I spun around and watched as the front doorknob turned. Then the door swung open.

In walked Paul and Leona Burhold. I waited, holding my breath. But no, that was all. No Tony! I breathed a sigh of relief.

"Hello!" said Paul, opening his arms wide to the collective diners.

Most everyone ignored him.

"Hey, if it isn't the king and queen of the universe," I whispered to Matt.

"Yeah, royalty are usually that popular," he said back.

I laughed.

They took a booth at the far end of the café, far from the next group of diners. That was out of character for them; they usually tried to be the center of attention.

Jeanette took them menus, but they didn't seem to want to order anything, just water. So Jeanette gathered the menus back and returned her pad to her hip pocket. Then she strolled back behind the counter.

While I downed another glass of water and nibbled

on Tom's salty roast beef sandwich, I watched Paul and Leona. I tried to read their lips, but I couldn't. They sat opposite each other in the booth, leaning forward like they were sharing secrets. Something was up.

We had finished eating, and Jeanette had cleared our table. Mom was getting ready to leave, searching her purse for her wallet, when a car pulled up in front of the Shamrock. It attracted no attention. It was a boring, brown, four-door missionary car. Nothing out of the ordinary. But it was almost too plain. I'd never seen the car before, but I had a feeling something was about to happen. So I stalled.

"What kind of pies do you have?" I asked Jeanette.

"Let's see," she said, standing on her tiptoes to peer into the twirling glass case. "One's a cherry. And this one's, um, cherry too. Looks like they're all cherry. I guess Tom made only one kind today."

"Cherry it is. Dessert's on me," I said. Mom and Matt looked at me, shocked.

"What?" I asked. "Can't I buy dessert for my loving family?"

Mom shrugged and put her purse back under the table. "None for me, thanks," she said.

"I'll have some, if he's paying," said Matt.

Then I remembered I was broke. "Yeah, sure. Can I borrow a couple of bucks, Mom?"

While we'd been ordering pie, a man had entered the café and was now sitting with the Burholds, beside Leona. They were all talking quietly, continuing the secret discussion.

Then Paul looked around and slowly took his notebook out of his pocket. He opened it, and the three began discussing its contents.

None of the other customers seemed to have even noticed the Burholds' guest come in. But why would they? He was superbly average, just like his car. He appeared to be average height. He had dull brown hair, wire-rimmed glasses, and the kind of pudgy face you could stare at for hours and not remember the next day.

It was so obvious.

"A spy," I whispered to myself. "They're all spies."

When we got home, I borrowed Mom's pickup, grabbed my binoculars, and raced back to the diner. The brown car was still out front. Through the café's cloudy window, I could see the blurry figures of Leona and Paul and the spy.

I waited in the truck for about twenty minutes, watching the Burholds and their friend through my binoculars.

Then Jeanette came out at the end of her shift.

She stuck her hands in her coat pockets and began walking toward home. I flashed my lights at her. She covered the side of her face from the glare and kept walking. I flashed the lights again, this time twice, but she kept walking.

She wasn't a very good spy.

I rolled down the window and yelled out, "Jeanette! Jeanette, it's me!"

She looked over. "Andrew? What are you doing out here?"

"Come 'ere."

She started to walk toward the truck but stopped a few feet in front, noticing my binoculars on the dashboard. "Have you been watching me?" she asked, wrinkling her nose.

"No! Come on, quick."

She didn't come on. She just folded her arms and tilted her head.

"I promise," I said. "I've been watching the Burholds and that *guy*."

She turned to look back in the café. Paul and Leona and the spy were putting on their coats. Jeanette unfolded her arms and dashed to the passenger side of the pickup.

"I was watching them too," she confided, pulling herself into the cab. "Who do you think that guy is?"

"I think he's a spy," I said as I rolled my window up.

Jeanette laughed.

"I'm serious. He's too average. I mean, nobody is that average-looking. And his car. It's average too."

"You watch too much TV," she said, but I could tell she was considering my idea.

"Look," I added, "no one knows what Tony's parents do, you know, for a job. They have money, but they don't ever leave town. You can't tell me you're not curious about them. They must be up to something."

"Like what?"

"I don't know, but I bet they're international terrorists or spies from some wacko country."

"Yeah, international terrorists usually show up in Spring Valley. I think they hold their annual convention here."

"You know a better place to hide?"

The three were leaving the diner.

"Duck," I said.

We peered over the dash and watched them get into their cars.

"Okay, let's follow 'em," said Jeanette, looking at me mischievously.

"Which car?" I asked.

"The other guy. The spy," said Jeanette.

"Good call."

The spy backed up and pulled out of the Shamrock parking lot before I started my engine and turned on my lights. I kept my eyes on the taillights and put Mom's truck into drive. I started edging out of my parking space when Jeanette screamed. I hit the brakes and saw the shocked and then smiling faces of Paul and Leona Burhold directly in front of us. They waved happily from their Mercedes that I'd almost sideswiped.

"Way to go," said Jeanette, slugging me on the shoulder. "I bet the CIA could use a guy like you."

"Sorry," I muttered.

"Come on, our cover's blown but we can still try to catch him. Pay attention!"

"Our cover's blown? Who watches too much TV?"

"Just move it."

We caught up to the brown four-door at the Gas-'n'-Go. I pulled over across the street in front of Irwin Gork's house, and we watched the scene from a respectable distance.

Irwin, the station owner, was standing by the spy's window. As usual, Irwin was paying more attention to a story he was telling than to the gas he was pumping. Irwin would talk to anyone who would listen. But he liked to talk to out-of-towners the most. People who didn't know him could be cornered and talked to for hours, if it was a slow night.

But either Irwin didn't have much to say, or the guy wasn't in the mood to be talked to. As soon as Irwin pulled the nozzle out of the tank, the spy handed over some money and peeled out of the station.

"Not too close," said Jeanette.

"I know what I'm doing," I replied. She snorted.

"Darn! He's leaving town," said Jeanette.

The spy's car pulled onto the freeway. I stopped on the shoulder, and we watched as the red taillights faded into the distance.

"Now what do we do?" I asked.

"Hmmm," said Jeanette.

"We could try the Burholds'," I said.

"Don't be an idiot."

"I'm not. They're up to something. I know it."

She let out a big sigh. "Let's just drive by their place." She pointed her finger at me. "But that's all."

"What you think I'm going to do, break into their house?"

"I don't know. You're acting weird again."

I swung the truck around and headed for the Burholds'.

We stopped up the road from their place, watching the tall house. Yellow lights glowed from one first-floor and one second-floor room. The Mercedes was in the garage, and the door was still up.

"You stay here," I whispered to Jeanette.

"Yeah, right."

"I'm serious. You stay."

"No way."

"Fine," I grumbled.

I grabbed my binoculars, and we ran to the bushes that edged the Burholds' property. Then we dropped to our knees and crawled along in the snow until we were parallel with the house. I pushed myself through the thorny hedge and then held the branches apart as Jeanette snuck through.

We crawled again until we reached the window with the light on. Jeanette stood up and looked in first, then pulled her head back quick.

"They're in there," she whispered.

"What are they doing?" I asked. My heart was beating so hard I was sure the Burholds would hear.

"Making an omelette. How should I know? I only looked for a second."

"Well, look again," I said helpfully.

She popped up again quickly. "They're at a computer."

I swallowed hard, then I pulled myself up and peered inside. It was a small room, full of tall bookshelves that held rows and rows of dusty blue and green books. Leona was seated at the computer typing. Paul was sitting beside her, looking over her shoulder and reading from the infamous notebook.

I dropped down from the window and pulled the binoculars off my shoulder.

"You going bird-watching?" asked Jeanette.

"No, wise guy. I'm going to read whatever's in that notebook or on their computer, maybe, if this works."

I carefully set the binoculars on the window ledge and began focusing the lens. Slowly a few blurry words started to appear on the computer's gray screen.

"Wow!" I said.

"What? What do you see?"

"Nothing. It's just real neat, that's all."

"Give me those," she snapped.

"No, I'm starting to get it. If only Leona'd move her . . . just a bit . . . yes."

I read word by word: *The town has developed a unique social strata, while the ethnic heritage, it seems, on the whole permeates from northern Europe. There are, of course, stereotypical examples of traditions that have continued from that region, and the previously stated anecdotal evidence tends to support our previously stated hypothesis. To gather more data, we must now move to the next level.*

I dropped down from the ledge and watched Jeanette shake her head. "They're spying on all of us, all right," she said.

"Spies!" I said too loudly.

"Shhh," she said. "I wonder what they mean by the next level? I bet that guy they met with tonight has something to do with it. You sure that was all there was on the screen?"

"Yeah."

She looked at me with distrust. "Let me see."

Jeanette pulled the binoculars from my hands. She stood up and brushed her knees off, bringing the binoculars up against the window with a thud.

A thud!

We dropped to the ground and looked at each other in shock. We started crawling back to the hedgerow, but within a few seconds I heard Tony's voice and saw the beams of a flashlight curving over the front lawn like prison spotlights. The light was headed for us, and we were trapped out in the open.

"Run," I yelled at Jeanette, jumping up. I changed direction and pumped my arms up and down in a race for the back hedge.

Jeanette was close on my heels. I pointed my shoulder and knifed my way through the hedgerow, not stopping to worry about the cuts I picked up. Jeanette followed, though not as fast. I finally ran back to help her through, and the hedge closed behind us just as the Burholds' back light flashed on.

We jumped a frozen ditch and then ran into a snow-covered field of weeds. I expected a bullet to whiz over my shoulder at any moment. I wondered what it would feel like to be shot. We ran for a long time, until we were sure no one was following.

Finally, we rested by a line of trees. "Do you think they saw us?" I asked, trying not to seem out of breath.

"No, they probably just thought they had a big bird stuck in their fence," answered Jeanette between gasps of air, her lips curled sarcastically. She seemed to be getting sarcastic and mean with me a lot lately.

We circled around to the truck, keeping as far away from the Burholds' as possible. A dog was barking at a nearby farmhouse, letting everyone know we were out in his field. So I kept on the lookout for Tony or one of his parents. But we made it back to the truck alone.

"Even if they did see us, I bet they don't know who it was," I said.

"Yeah, probably. Hey, my coat snagged," muttered Jeanette.

"Sorry." I didn't mention that I had cuts all over my hands from my lunge through the hedge.

"You sure there wasn't anything else on the computer?" Jeanette asked again as I started the pickup and pulled away from the curb.

"I told you, it was just a bunch of stuff about Spring Valley's ethnic background or something. And then that they were going to move to the next level."

"That's all you remember?" she asked.

"Like I said, they had a hypothesis, just like science class. And then it said they were moving to the next level."

"They're studying us, I'm sure about that," said Jeanette. "They're after something."

"Yeah," I said.

Then I hit the brakes in a panic. "Hey, where're my binoculars?"

"I don't know. I thought you had them."

"Why would I have them? You were holding them."

She shrugged.

"Geez, you lost my binoculars," I said.

"I want to go home," said Jeanette.

———

I couldn't sleep that night, dreaming up horrible consequences for our spying. If the Burholds had seen us, they would most likely slip into my room and shoot me with a silencer or smother me with a pillow. If Tony had seen us, he'd probably beat me up at school.

I didn't know which would be worse.

———

It snowed again overnight. But as Matt and I carried our books out to his Duster that Tuesday, the temperature had dropped to bitter depths, too cold to snow anymore. He had the block heater plugged in, but the Duster looked like a big red block of ice and I couldn't imagine it starting. Breathing in through his mouth, Matt pushed the key into the ignition and turned.

Click, answered by a bad word from Matt. Another turn. The engine cranked heavily, slowly. Then stopped. Another bad word from Matt. Another turn. The engine fired once.

"Yes!" Matt said, gripping the steering wheel firmly with his left hand as if the car might surge at any moment and race out of the driveway.

The engine turned again and fired again, and this time it kept firing. He nursed the gas pedal as the engine grudgingly began to rumble at a normal pace.

Our tires crunched over the new snow as we pulled onto the road. No one had driven our road yet, and the snow had been disturbed only by the erratic dance of Mrs. Thomas's two collies out for their morning adventure. Our snowplow operator never got out to clear our road before nine o'clock after a weekday storm. And he'd even wait until ten on weekends.

As we drove, I hugged myself to keep warm against the bitter cold. Matt was warm, but then again he was dressed for the cold. Matt didn't care about looking cool; he just *was* cool. He wore a scarf, gloves, parka, the whole nerd ball game. I wore my jean jacket over a T-shirt and shivered on the passenger side, feeling like a side of beef in transport. It wasn't a long ride, but the car heater never warmed up enough for us to actually know it was on.

He pulled the Duster onto Second Street while struggling for something to say to fill the silence. I did not want to talk. I was too worried about Tony and his terrorist parents. Also, I was still depressed about Jeanette.

As she had made clear on our balloon ride, we weren't really going out as boyfriend and girlfriend. She hadn't even kissed me. And yet I couldn't get her off my mind.

But as we neared the school, I realized it was Tony I was most concerned about. Would he be waiting for me? Had he seen me?

Matt started to open his mouth to speak again. My mind raced for something to say to keep him from asking about Jeanette or Tony. I had my history book in my lap. We were studying European history.

"I bet it was colder than this in the Dark Ages," I said, pulling my jean jacket tight around my neck. It was all I could think of to start a conversation.

Matt looked at me blankly.

"Well," I added. "It was the Dark Ages—gloomy, you know."

"All these years I thought I was the strange one in the family," Matt said back, smiling.

"What'd I say?"

"Nothing, Plato. It was reeeeal deep."

Matt pulled his scarf away from his mouth. "It's so cold that if the Constitution had been written here today, they would have started *We the Popsicles.*" Matt never allowed anyone to be weirder than he was, and I laughed at his lousy joke.

I should say Matt never let anyone be weirder than he was except for that Saturday—but I suppose we'll get to that soon enough.

When we pulled into the school parking lot, I pushed myself straight up in the seat to look over the assorted cars parked by the side door.

No sign of Tony's Mercedes or of Jeanette. I scanned the entire lot. Nothing.

It felt good to get into the warmth of school. I got to my locker and put my books away before the first bell rang. I waited, but still no sign of Tony. I kept my eyes fixed on his locker as if he might pop out of it at any second.

I was in a trance, still staring, when I felt warm air on my neck. I turned slowly to look into Tony Burhold's cold eyes and dark, bushy eyebrows. His immense face was tensed up so tight we could have used his forehead as a bicycle rack. He *must* have seen me peeking into his house.

As he looked over at me, I remembered a pamphlet a ranger gave us at Yellowstone Park. It told us that if we were attacked by a bear, we should play dead. *Yes, I will play dead,* my fevered mind thought.

"Hey, Tony," I said in a tone that probably translated into *Don't hurt me, Tony.*

He breathed out again. "I don't like you, Stenson," he said deeply, then he crossed his arms over his thick chest and drew in a big breath.

"What'd I do?" I asked, backing up a step and putting my hand casually against my locker. I wanted to be tough, to stick up to this guy, but he was just so darn big, and he had this crazed look in his eyes as if he didn't care if he went to jail for a long time. Anyway, Jeanette wasn't around. No point in getting killed when no one was there to see me put up a good fight. She would just hear the outcome in English class. "Did you hear Tony turned Andrew into creamed tuna this morning?" Lisa or one of her other friends would tell her.

Tony didn't answer my question. He just looked around the halls, chewing a wad of green gum that he occasionally pushed in and out of his mouth with his tongue. People passed, but no one stopped to see what was going on, to help me. No one would even look at us.

I thought about what I should say next. Okay, he probably knew it was me outside his house. But still there was a chance he didn't. I picked my words with as much care as Mom choosing early-summer tomatoes at the IGA.

"This about last night?" I asked him. There, that was vague enough.

He brought his big hand up to rub the stubble on his chin. He was sixteen, maybe seventeen, and had thick, dark stubble like some guy in a razor commercial! But the rubbing meant the question had confused him, obviously.

"What?"

"Oh, nothing." Okay, he hadn't seen me. So then what was this about?

"You know, in karate they teach us to break bones."

It was Matt's voice. Matt was here to back me up! His skinny frame was hidden behind the hulking figure of Tony, so I couldn't see him very well; Tony was as wide as a pop machine. But still, I had help.

Matt, of course, had never taken a karate lesson in his life, but we'd heard that line in a Chuck Norris movie we'd rented. At the time we both agreed that it was a line we'd have to use one day.

Tony stepped farther into the hallway so he could look at both of us. "You two girls want to fight or something?" he asked slowly.

"Huh? Oh, I wasn't talking to you," said Matt with mock surprise. "I didn't even see you there. Tony Bur-*head,* isn't it?"

81

"Burhold," he said back flatly.

"Yeah. Anyway, Andrew and I need to get to class. We'd love to stay and talk, but something tells me it would be a one-sided conversation." Matt pushed me down the hall.

"You're not going to see her again," Tony said calmly as we walked away.

We stopped about ten feet from Tony and his mighty, wrinkled forehead.

"What?" I asked, amazed. I'd heard him, but it caught me unprepared. This wasn't about me peeking into his house; this was the long-awaited confrontation about Jeanette. I'd rehearsed this meeting a hundred times in my head, but now with scary Tony in front of me I didn't know what to say.

"You're not gonna see Jenny again," he repeated.

Matt turned to me and asked, "Did you hear that, Andrew? You're not going to see her again. Tony must be a magician, and he's going to make Jeanette disappear!"

I couldn't help laughing nervously.

"You know what I mean, you dweebs," Tony said to us. I stopped laughing. "You're not going to go out with Jenny again *or* talk to her. You get it?"

I had to stand up to this guy.

"You get it?" he asked again. Matt and Tony were looking at me. At that moment it seemed everyone in the halls was looking at me. I couldn't let him push me around like that.

"Yeah, I guess," I whispered. Matt breathed out in a disappointed kind of *whoosh*. Tony unwrinkled his brow and brushed past us toward his locker. I'd folded as quick as Superman on wash day.

Matt whacked his palm on the back of my head.

"All right," I whispered.

"No! I don't get it," I called out to Tony's back. Tony stopped and turned around.

"You and Jeanette aren't going out. And you can't tell me who I can talk to or go out with, you get it?"

Tony didn't have time to answer.

"Keep moving, boys." It was our principal, Mr. Walker. He reached up and put one of his skinny hands on Tony's shoulder.

"Got class. Don't want to be late." As always, Principal Walker was speaking in short, choppy sentences.

No one moved. "Problem here?" he asked.

"Nope," said Tony, and he started walking backward down the hall.

"Fine," said Walker. "Hurry, boys, hurry."

"You had to do it," said Matt, pulling me to drama class. "He may crush you like a bug tomorrow, but today you stood up to him."

———

For the next couple of days I kept looking over my shoulder. At school I was afraid to go into the bathroom alone for fear Tony was hiding in a stall waiting for me. At home I still couldn't sleep. Every time I drifted off, I woke with a start, thinking a rustling at the window was Paul Burhold in a ski mask.

But Tony just ignored me as usual. And the Burholds didn't come to get me. So I decided to go after them.

———

One evening just after dark, I drove to the Burholds' and parked. I waited while the truck cab grew colder and colder. Finally, just when I was about to give in and run the heater for a while, their garage-door opener began to groan and the door slowly rolled up. From the dark garage, headlights flashed on and two figures pulled out in the Mercedes. I fired up the truck and followed, not putting on my headlights until their car was almost out of sight.

"Smooth," I said, congratulating myself.

They drove slowly on the slick roads out onto Second and then left on Montana Avenue. They went only a block on Montana before pulling over and getting out. I climbed out of the truck and followed Paul and Leona on foot, dashing from pine tree to pine tree as they strolled by the houses, pausing now and then to look around.

When we were nearing the Presbyterian church on the corner, I ducked behind a bush to give them time to cross the road. But when I peered out again they had disappeared.

Had they seen me? Were they hiding and waiting for me to make a move? I was ready to run when I heard a distant "Ouch!" It was Paul's voice.

I dropped to the ground and shuffled along on elbows and knees until I could see them. They were on the church grounds. Leona was walking around a big, snow-covered rock. Paul was hopping on one foot while rubbing the other; he must have stubbed it in the dark.

Leona said something to Paul, and he stopped hopping and they both moved to the back of the church. Then they cupped their hands to the sides of their faces and began peering in through a long window.

"Now I've got you," I mumbled.

Faintly I could hear singing, the stopping and starting voices of a choir practicing.

"But why are you spying on choir practice?" I said aloud. Maybe they were casing the place, planning to come back and rob it later. Maybe they were just weird. It didn't make much sense, but it was probably illegal. If I called Dad, he might arrest them. That would be embarrassing to Tony. But I needed more. I needed enough to get the Burholds to leave town in shame. So I waited.

They stayed glued to the window for about fifteen minutes, then they whispered to each other and returned to the road. Under the light of the streetlamp, Paul scribbled a few notes in his book.

I stayed hidden behind a tree until they walked by. In fact, I had to wait for them to get into their car and drive past before I could safely get up and race back to the truck. By the time I got my frozen limbs running and then got the truck started and in gear, they were out of sight. At Second Street, with deserted roads in either direction, I had to take a chance. I turned left, toward downtown.

I sped through the dark streets of the business district, but the Mercedes was gone. In a panic I headed north to the Ridgemont suburbs and cruised those streets. Still no luck. Then I tried the west end, but no Burholds. Precious time was wasting, but I had no idea where they could have gone.

Had they gone home? Had they left town?

And then it hit me.

"Of course," I said aloud. "The lodge."

———

About a million years ago, before my family moved to town, the Spring Valley lodge building had been the concession stand of a drive-in theater. Eventually the theater went out of business, and the lodge members had swooped in with a bag of money and bought the isolated theater, renovating the concession stand into their lodge hall.

I'd never been in the lodge. None of my friends and few of their parents had either. No kids and no newcomers, those were the main rules.

Still, I didn't know why anyone would want to go there. The lodge hall itself sat in the middle of the deserted drive-in parking lot. The building's cedar paneling was falling off and had been replaced with patches of linoleum and plywood and anything else that had been handy. The roof of rusting tin had been patched a dozen times through the years with great gobs of tar. Surrounding the lodge were a few remaining speaker poles looking ominously like impaled heads left by savages.

By my estimation, it was the scariest-looking place I could imagine.

As kids Matt and I had snuck out there a couple of times. Once we'd gotten brave enough to go up to the back door and listen to the eerie laughter of the men inside. Another time, just after we'd jumped the fence the back door had started to open and we'd screamed and ran all the way home.

Like a lot of people in the valley, I didn't know much about the lodge meetings. But I knew they were held on this night. And I knew there would be a lot of well-to-do business people there.

Again, I could only imagine what the Burholds had in mind. Robbery? Kidnapping? Murder?

———

The Burholds had parked out front. It was a bold move, but wise. Who'd notice a Mercedes amid the other fancy cars? I parked outside the lot and watched for signs of movement around the building. Nothing. So I got out and made a wide circle of the outside of the dark lot, walking just inside the fence. As I walked I kept my eyes fixed on the building. But after the long loop, I had seen no Burholds, no movement. They must be inside. But how? The lodge would never let the Burholds inside; they were newcomers. Worse, they were newcomers who asked a lot of questions.

They must have broken in.

I moved closer and skirted the building again, looking for an open window the Burholds may have used. Instead I picked up the trail of two sets of footprints in the snow, one large and the other small. Impressed by my brilliance, I followed the trail to the back door. I tried the handle. It was unlocked.

Slowly I pulled the door open. It creaked a little but then gave quietly. I stuck my head inside and received a face full of smoke and then, a second later, an ear full of distant laughter. The door opened onto an empty hallway. I stepped inside and pulled the door closed behind me.

Ahead, the hallway twisted out of sight but obviously led to the lodge meeting, where I could hear voices and laughter. To the left a door was ajar. Through the crack I could hear dishes rattling; it was probably the kitchen. To the right a decrepit flight of stairs rose.

The Burholds had come in this way, obviously. They then had to make a decision, I reasoned. "If I were the Burholds, where would I go?" I whispered to myself. Lodge members were to the left and in front.

"Upstairs, of course," I said.

I quietly placed my snow-covered running shoe on the first step. *Grooooan, creeeeak.*

I stepped down quickly, and the hideous noise stopped.

The laughter had stopped in the front room. The dishes had stopped rattling in the kitchen. I held my breath and prepared to run, but soon the voices began talking again. Then more laughter came.

I lifted my foot higher and tried the second step, placing it far to the edge. It made only a little sound. I moved my weight onto it and tried the next step. One by one I climbed the stairs, stepping lightly on the edges. Finally I reached a turn in the staircase.

I made the turn and kept moving. Ten more steps. I quickened my pace. What would I do when I found them? Yell probably and then let the lodge members deal with them. It was gonna be great. Finally I stepped into the black attic and looked around for a light switch. But as I took my weight off the last step, the dry, old staircase let out a hideous, ear-splitting *Raaaaarch! Craaack!*

Downstairs the laughter quieted a bit.

"That Billy?" a familiar voice called out from the main hall. I knew the voice, but from where?

"Billy?" the voice asked again.

"Nope, that ain't me," said Billy. "I was in the kitchen."

Silence downstairs. I wondered what to do.

Then I heard footsteps. Suddenly someone was at the bottom of the stairs.

Before I could move, a figure had bounded up the stairs and moved behind me. His hand was on my shoulder. I spun around and looked down into the glassy eyes of a beaver. No, I looked farther down. It was somebody in a beaver hat. It was Principal Walker.

"Oh, no," I grumbled.

"Stenson!" he said, raising his eyebrows, which made the beaver rise at the same time. "Typical."

"No, you don't understand."

He wasn't in a listening mood. He grabbed my ear and pulled me down the stairs. In a few bounds we were in the hall, walking a gauntlet of lodge members in beaver hats. We rounded the bend in the hallway, and he pushed me into the middle of the main room. The lodge was much nicer inside than outside, decorated with rustic shotguns and Western art and surrounded by roaring fireplaces and big, comfy chairs.

"They'll get away!" I finally said, looking at Walker. But he was too mad to listen.

I turned to one of the other members, who I didn't recognize. "They're up there," I said, pointing up.

"Let's gag him," the guy suggested, grabbing the knot in his tie and moving it back and forth like a goon in a gangster movie.

"But—"

The man started to move closer, and I closed my mouth tightly.

"Strict punishment breaking and entering," said Walker, regaining some of his composure. He smoothed his pants and sat on a log chair near one of the fireplaces. "Ten years jail probably do you good."

"Then *they* go to jail too," I spat out.

"Who?" he said, leaning forward.

"The ones I've been telling you about. The Burholds."

"What?" said Walker.

"Newcomers?" asked the other guy.

"They're here," I said. "Their car's out front. I followed their tracks to the back."

Walker leaned back in the chair and then forward again. Obviously he wasn't expecting this excuse. He didn't know whether to believe me or not.

"I'm not lying," I said.

"Come on," he said, pushing himself up. He strode out of the main hall, and I followed. He took the stairs two at a time. Oddly, they didn't make a sound that way.

At the top he reached behind a pillar and flicked on the light.

"Well?" he said.

"Geez," I muttered. There was nothing up there. It was just a big, empty, dusty attic. "They must have gotten away," I said pathetically.

"You won't," said Walker as he reached for my ear.

"But they were here, I'm sure of it," I said.

"We *could* look in the storage closet," someone suggested.

"Yeah," I agreed, pulling away from Walker's ear grip. "Let's look. Where is it? Is it up here? I'll look."

Walker rolled his eyes, let out a breath, and strode over to the far end of the attic. Without pausing, he turned the knob and pulled open the door. He didn't even bother to look inside.

"Big trouble," Walker said to me.

But I wasn't going to be in big trouble. Because inside the closet something was moving—two somethings were moving.

"Hello!" said Paul Burhold in his booming, confident voice.

"Yes!" I said. "Someone get a rope."

CHAPTER 9

It Was Matt's Idea

I'm an idiot," I said to Matt late that night.

"Yes, what's your point?"

"Tomorrow, Tony Burhold is going to be a bigger hero than ever." I flopped down on Matt's bed and covered my head with his pillow.

"Why, did he figure out how to read?"

"Funny you should say that," I said, lifting up the pillow. "It seems his mom and dad know how to read. And write."

"Yeah?" said Matt, waiting for more.

"Tonight I found out what they do for a living. So did a lot of other people."

"Oh yeah?" Matt was interested, and he didn't get interested very often.

"I followed them," I started.

"Bright idea," said Matt sarcastically.

"It seemed like a good idea at the time. Anyway, I followed them to the lodge meeting."

"Hmmm," said Matt.

"That's exactly what I thought. They snuck in and I followed them, but Walker caught me."

"As in Principal Walker?"

"Yeah, that's the guy. And just when Walker and his buddies are about to roast me in their fire for spying, I tell them I followed the Burholds there. So we go upstairs to the attic, and there are the Burholds hiding in a closet."

"Interesting."

"Yeah. Anyway, Paul walks out of the closet all full of smiles like he's Santa arriving at the mall."

"I can see that."

"But everyone is really mad. And I'm thinking, *This is the end of Tony Burhold.* But then Leona walks out of the closet, and she's holding something up. And we all walk closer and see that it's a book. A book with Paul and Leona's names on it. A book that's called *Life in America's Small Towns,* volume four."

"Paul and Leona wrote a book?"

"Oh yeah, many books. It seems they've lived in different small towns across the country. And they like to watch people, even spy, before letting on who they are."

"So that we all act natural," said Matt.

"That's the idea," I answered. "Remember that guy in the café the other day? The guy talking to the Burholds?"

"I don't know. Maybe."

"Well, Jeanette and I thought he was a spy. But it turns out he's their editor from New York. And he gave them the go-ahead to do a book on Spring Valley."

"Wow!" said Matt. "So Walker and the rest of them weren't mad anymore?"

I scoffed. "Walker grabbed their arms and led them down to the main room and got them all comfortable and had someone bring 'em food. When I left, the lodge members were falling all over themselves telling stories and asking if they wanted anything else to eat or drink. It made me sick."

"Interesting," was all Matt could think to say.

———

Jeanette was already in her seat when I got to Mrs. Curry's English class on Thursday morning. Tony wasn't there yet.

"Yo!" I said, bobbing my head and doing a subtle Tony impression.

"You get smarter or something?" Jeanette asked me as I sat in the seat next to her.

"Ha. Why?"

"You don't have any books."

Geez. In my haste to get to class before Tony, I'd run from drama class so fast that I'd forgotten to get my books.

"Oh, I don't need any books. I've memorized them all. When you have a photographic memory like I do, you can do that."

But my face was stop-sign red. I knew I should go back to my locker, but I really didn't want anyone to tell her about Tony's parents before I had a chance to ask her out for the weekend.

"I guess I'd better go get a book or two, just for appearances. So the rest of you don't resent my genius."

"Very generous of you," said Jeanette as she ran her fingers slowly through her long hair.

"Hey," I asked as I got up, pretending it was a spontaneous thought. "You're coming out again Saturday night, right? I have a game, but it'll be over by eight or so. And it's always a creative thrill a minute when you're out with me, huh?"

"Well, Andrew," she said, "um, there's something I need to tell you."

She wasn't looking at me but down at *Catcher in the Rye* on her desk. She bit her bottom lip and flipped aimlessly through the pages. It wasn't like her to be coy, and after a second of this distracted behavior she seemed to realize that too.

"Tony already asked me to go to the game on Saturday night, and he wants me to go out after with his parents. I can't really say no after . . . well, after finding out about Paul and Leona. One of my dad's friends called last night and told us what happened at the lodge meeting. You hear about that? And I thought it might be kind of fun to be included in the Burholds' book. And anyway you hadn't asked me, and we aren't exactly going out seriously or anything, so I didn't think you would mind."

Arrrrrgh! I couldn't catch my breath. My eyes were glowing like a demon from a Stephen King movie. Why hadn't I left the Burholds alone?

"Let's go somewhere and talk," I said, doing my best to control the half of me that wanted to start bawling. The other half of me wanted to jump up and down and kick my desk into a pile of broken wood.

She held up her hand as if she were carrying a tray waitress-style. "Class is going to start. We can't go."

"Just for a minute, please," I begged.

"No, Andrew. I can't."

My heart was squashed. I couldn't even bring myself to get up and fetch my books. Then Mrs. Curry walked in, and I was forced to sit as inconspicuously as possible so she wouldn't call on me to read or answer a question.

It was in that classroom, as I sat in misery while the others contemplated *Catcher in the Rye,* that I realized I needed a plan.

My inability to win Jeanette over, and now the latest Tony developments, called for drastic measures. Sure, I had to ask Jeanette to be my girlfriend. But I needed more than that now. On Saturday night, she would see a chiseled Tony Burhold in a tank top score twenty points and steal the show at the game. Then she would go out with the Burholds and tell them her life story. Of course, after that she would start seeing Tony seriously because she wouldn't want to do anything to be left out of the book.

I needed to do something to convince her that Tony was an unimaginative gorilla, the Burholds' book was passé, and I was the only guy for her. I needed something creative and charming.

As I walked out of school that afternoon, I was in a trance. My brain raced for a plan that would win Jeanette.

That night I took one of our horses, Sweet Pea, on a ride down the road to Jeanette's just to see if Tony's Mercedes was there. It wasn't. But I still couldn't bring myself to knock on her door.

When I brought Sweet Pea back, I worked her over with the currycomb until her black coat shone. She liked the attention.

"Try and stay clean," I told her and patted her on the side.

I jogged into the house and up the stairs. Matt heard me and yelled out.

"Thinking of joining the rodeo?" he asked and laughed at his own joke. He was lying on his bed filling out this week's sweepstakes forms.

"Yeah," I answered. "And you can be the clown. You've already got the big nose and floppy feet."

"You're pretty hilarious for a guy who's gonna lose his girl to Tony Burhead," said Matt.

"Aw, shuddup." I sat on the end of Matt's bed and let out a huge sigh.

"Is there a chance you want me to ask what's wrong now?" he asked.

"You know, I'm actually desperate enough to come to you again."

"Golly, could this be about Jenny—I mean Jeanette?" he said sarcastically.

"Just forget it."

"Now don't be touchy. Let's see what we can think up."

I leaned forward and put my face in my hands. "Uff," I grunted.

"What?" asked Matt.

"Nothing. I don't know. I need something really big

this time. I need something to really impress Jeanette before our game on Saturday. She's coming to the game. And then she and Tony and the Hemingways are going out after."

"So you want to stop this?" asked Matt.

"I was thinking that if Jeanette and I were going out steady, she wouldn't want to go out with Tony or even be in the Burholds' book. You think?"

"Could be," answered Matt, though he didn't sound like he meant it.

Matt went back to his sweepstakes forms, and I leaned back on the bed.

After a few minutes Matt clapped his hands as if he were leaving a football huddle. "How about a show of affection?"

"Hmmph. What?"

"Okay, picture this. You're Jeanette. You're sitting in the stands before the game. Down on the floor are the two guys vying for your attention. One's a hunk with famous parents and the other—well, he's creative."

Matt made a sweeping gesture with his arm. "When out of the sky drops a banner pronouncing Andrew Stenson's undying love. The crowd roars, the other players slap you on the back, Jeanette faints with the excitement. I bet she wouldn't even look at Tony after that. And I bet you'd be included in the Burholds' book."

I sat still for a while thinking, trying not to break into too big a grin. A banner! It was a good idea.

"What do you think?" asked Matt.

"I like it," I admitted, grinning like a fool.

He laughed. "Then it's certain?"

"What?"

"That you've completely lost all reason."

"Why?"

"Because I was kidding. That won't impress her; it'll embarrass her."

"Ah, what do you know?"

"More than you, that's for sure."

But I wasn't listening anymore. I was thinking about the banner. It was a good idea. Forget that, it was a *great* idea. Dare I say brilliant?

———

Our team played an away game in Glasgow on Friday evening. We needed to win the game and the one on Saturday to have even a chance of making the state playoffs.

No Spring Valley team had beat a Glasgow team since the dawn of time. Glasgow High had more students, sure. But it was more than that. The kids in Glasgow lived to play basketball. And they played it with a frightening obsession. In fact, Glasgow hadn't lost a home game to anyone in three years.

But what happened that night would change basketball history in Spring Valley. It also would convince me I needed to go through with my plan for Saturday's game. I needed something big to win Jeanette's heart.

— CHAPTER 10 —

57

The sky was gray, and it was snowing lightly as the team bus reached the edge of Glasgow. The bus slowed, and as we turned into the parking lot we all stared through the windows at the school's tall gym. Out of the building's high horizontal windows streamed yellow, flickering light.

I was sitting in the front of the bus—as far away from Tony as I could—with my nose pressed to the window. Through the steam of my breath, I imagined the gym packed with chanting Glasgow fans. They always drew a large crowd for their games. In Spring Valley, we had never attracted anyone to our games. But of course all that was changing with the amazing Tony Burhold in the lineup. People wanted to see Tony play. And now even Jeanette wanted to see Tony play.

I sat back and looked down the aisle of the bus. Wayne, our starting point guard, had his stumpy, hairy legs stretched out in the seat across from me. He had on headphones and was moving his head slowly up and down to the music. In the seat behind him sat Joe, a happy guy, all elbows and pointy shoulders. He told me he had once been stopped by a mall detective who suspected he was walking out of the store with some article of clothing stuck under his shirt, still attached to a pointy coat hanger. I don't know if he was telling the truth, but it was a good story. Anyway, Joe was a reserve forward. And like me he rarely played.

Two empty rows and then Tony, my competition in the great race for Jeanette McCaffrey's affection. I wasn't a short kid by any means, but Tony was another two or three inches taller than I was. I wasn't that bad an athlete, but Tony was twice the jock. He could jump from under the basket, spin completely around, and stuff the basketball with one of his big, meaty hands. The following *thung!* would seem to resound throughout the gym for a full minute. He could shoot jump shots with either hand and fake with such speed and apparent ease that he could turn you around in your shorts.

He could—oops, he was looking at me, and he'd caught me staring. I quickly turned away and slumped down into my seat.

The bus came to a hissing stop in front of the gym. What little daylight there was had disappeared to the west. The only light was coming from the gym's high windows. I didn't know it at the time, but inside the place Tony Burhold would make state basketball history.

Horns started blaring as we dressed in the locker room.

"Geez, Tony," Joe was saying. "Put your shoes on. Your socks stink."

Tony jumped up, grabbed Joe around the neck, and stuck his big shoe in Joe's face.

"Ugggh!" yelled Joe, pushing Tony away. But it was obvious Joe liked being teased by the great Tony Burhold. Tony was laughing a big laugh that came from deep inside his cavernous chest.

The rest of us watched him. It was also obvious that Tony liked Joe. But the fact that Joe was a reserve, like me, stung a little. Maybe Tony was just pretending to like him so I'd feel even more alienated.

"Come on, you girls," barked Tony. "Let's kick some butt."

The rest of the team cheered and jumped up. The coach had been getting ready to say something, but he stood aside as Tony ran us onto the Glasgow gym floor. The crowd met us with a thundering boo, and we fell in behind Tony as if he were a tank leading us into battle.

After a quick warm-up I took my seat, the best in the house to witness what many would call Spring Valley's only basketball miracle.

The ref threw the ball up, and Tony slapped it back to Wayne, who faded left then right and then sprinted up the floor. "Glassssgow! Glllassssssgow!" yelled the crowd. The Glasgow defenders seemed to be everywhere, jumping up and down and waving their arms like mad apes.

Wayne held his cool and fired around the perimeter to Greg. Tony was posting up in the lane, so Greg floated a pass over the excited Glasgow arms. "Glassssgow! Glllasssss-gow!" the crowd yelled again. Tony was the only person in the building who wasn't listening. He was eight feet from the basket when he got the ball. He palmed it, took two quick, powerful steps—splitting a pair of defenders—and exploded like an Olympic high jumper. He soared higher than I'd ever seen him before and jammed the ball hard through the rim.

Silence from the crowd.

Glasgow inbounded, and their point man quickly brought the ball up court. He paused at the top of the key and then dished off to their big man underneath. Greg, our power forward, was guarding him. The Glasgow guy pulled back and sent an off-balance ten-footer toward the basket. Suddenly there was Tony, floating above the court and—*slap!*—blocking the shot. The ball ended up in the stands. Somehow the crowd got even quieter than before.

Glasgow sent the ball in, but Wayne intercepted and

sent a lob up to Jim, who was breaking for the far basket. Jim took the pass at midcourt, dribbled to his weak side, and threw the ball off the backboard. Tony, trailing the play, jumped, caught the ball in his left hand, and slammed it through the net with a hammer-like blow.

Our bench went wild. We were up four to nothing on the best high school basketball team in the state. I pretended to cheer.

As Glasgow brought the ball up court, Joe turned to me and said, "How about that Tony?" Then he added, "Hey, you hear about his parents?"

I grunted and hoped Tony would fall on his face.

———

No such luck. It was Tony's game. Glasgow could not contain our star, and he played like a one-man team.

Just before the halftime buzzer, Wayne tried a desperation shot from midcourt that hit the rim but then bounced harmlessly over the backboard. Everyone in the gym looked up in unison at the scoreboard. Home 19, Visitor 40.

My bench-warming mate, Joe, patted me on the back, and I accepted it as if I had actually contributed to the lopsided Spring Valley lead.

Everyone made way for Tony as he strode into the locker room. He slumped down on a bench and wrapped a towel around his neck. I stared at him, trying to soak in the fact that Tony Burhold had just scored thirty-four of our forty first-half points. He had already demolished our school record for points in a game. At this rate he might just set the state record for points, whatever it was.

"Andrew," Coach said to me. "You, Joe, and Chris can start the second half."

I looked incredulously at Coach and then over at Tony, who was shaking his head and half-grinning at me. It was not a nice kind of grin.

"Steve, Wayne, and Tony, you sit for a few minutes. You've earned the rest," added Coach.

Glasgow inbounded the ball to start the second half. I stuck as close as possible to my man, their backup center, a tall, lanky kid wearing number seventeen. But he was fast and could stop and start quicker than Mrs. Thomas's collies. Their point man got him the ball, and he sliced past me and floated a ten-footer up and off the side of the rim. It was a pretty shot, and it dropped through the net easily. Jim inbounded to Chris, who slowed the tempo and dribbled smoothly up court.

"Hey, moron!" Tony yelled to me as I ran past the bench. "If you can't stop seventeen, get off the floor!" I looked ahead and swallowed hard.

We passed the ball around the perimeter, and then I lobbed it in to Joe, who was posting up inside. I thanked the basketball gods for letting the pass make it to my bench-warming partner, who faked, jumped a few inches, and banked a poor shot off the backboard and back into the mass of flailing Glasgow arms.

We raced backcourt to be ready for Glasgow. This time I was glued to my man, and Glasgow went to the other side for their shot. *Swish.* Then we were on offense again.

A couple of plays flew by before I was in a position to shoot. Glasgow was giving me room inside the paint, and Chris got me the ball. I spun and let fly an awkward hook shot. The ball sailed high and came down heavy on the front of the rim, *thunk,* hit the backboard, *smack,* and floated awkwardly in midair for a long, long second before finally dropping through the net, *floosh.*

I jumped into the air and yelled, "Yes!"

I'd never netted a hook shot in a real game.

We gave it all we had. But despite my bucket and a three-pointer Chris dropped in, Glasgow outscored us fourteen to five before Coach pulled the reserves. I'd managed to keep the center I was defending to four points, but I had picked up a handful of fouls in the process.

I wiped my forehead and looked up at the scoreboard. Glasgow 33, Visitors 45.

Glasgow was pumped up by their rally, but Tony was back on the court. He grabbed the inbound pass from Garrett and brought it up court himself. Tony didn't pause when he reached their front line of defense; he threw a quick head fake and charged through the Glasgow players as if they were dry pine and he was a ten-pound axe handle. Tony easily laid up what would be the first two of his twenty-three second-half points.

———

A mad Glasgow fan had done it, of course. But we all understood that it was a sign of acknowledgment.

A fan who had witnessed greatness in the gym had spray-painted a black 57 on the side of our bus. Fifty-seven points by one player in a high school basketball game was unheard of in Montana. Especially against a powerhouse like Glasgow. I knew it. Everyone knew it.

We stood aside while Tony approached the bus. He walked slowly from the back and ran his hand along the side, through the wet paint. Then he pushed his palm against the bus, leaving a black handprint, and got on board.

As the Spring Valley basketball team drove out of town with the black, smeared 57 dripping down the side of the bus, I realized they would never forget Tony Burhold in Glasgow. Just as they will never forget me in Spring Valley. But for very, very different reasons.

After that night, of course, there was no way I would lose the courage to go through with *the plan:* to win Jeanette before we played a team nowhere near as good as Glasgow.

With Jeanette in the crowd, Tony would quickly net 239 points and we'd get a big enough lead for Coach to put me in. With Jeanette there, I wouldn't hit a hook shot. I'd probably end up bouncing the ball off my foot and air-balling two shots and be pulled. Jeanette and the rest of the crowd would laugh at me, and Paul Burhold would make note of it in his book. Tony would come back in and score another eight hundred points, flex his muscles, and be an even bigger hero.

On Saturday morning, I got up early, even before Mom, and fed Sweet Pea and Blaze. I slipped into Matt's room and pulled his keys out of his jean pocket without jingling them and without waking him. I was too nervous to eat, so I gulped down a swig of milk and left by the back door. It was still very dark, very cold.

Despite the early-morning cold, the old Duster fired up on the first turn as if it were eager to take me into town and as curious as I was about my ultimate destiny. Within a few minutes I was on the road, rumbling north. The dawn was breaking to my right.

I pulled down Main Street well before any of the stores were open and had to sit shivering in the car until the hardware store opened at eight. A mustached guy not much older than I was finally unlocked the front doors and then pushed a snowblower outside for display.

"Not many people greet me on a Saturday morn," he said as I jumped out of the car. "What can I get ya?"

"I need some wire, some thick stuff. Two twenty-five-foot lengths. And then a long piece, thinner, maybe a hundred feet of that. Then a really big sheet of white paper or something like that. And a can of red paint, not too much."

"Hmmm. Okay."

Riiinng. Darn, the phone was ringing. Mr. Mustache sauntered over to answer it.

"Yo," he said. Then there was silence for about a minute. Then he proceeded to nod and grunt into the mouthpiece for another five minutes.

I began pacing in front of him, giving him dirty looks. I had work to do! But he didn't notice or didn't care that I was impatient.

Finally I gave up and rounded up the stuff for the banner myself. I handed over the last of my money, and well before nine I was ready to head back home.

As I walked to the Duster with my heavy, clinking bag, I made the time calculations in my head. Fifteen minutes to home, a couple of hours to get the banner painted and put together, and then another couple of hours to set it up before the first spectators started arriving at the gym. No problem.

I turned the key in the Duster. Not even a click. Dead. Beyond dead. The Duster had *decomposed.*

I did the first logical thing that crossed my mind: I panicked. First I hit the dashboard with my fist. That didn't help, so I pushed myself out of the car and into the cold morning. I popped the hood and twisted wires, pulled important-looking cables. Then I jumped back into the car and turned the key again. Still nothing. More fiddling with multicolored wires. I even looked for a big on-off switch. Still no spark.

I stood beside the car with booster cables in hand as an assorted group of shoppers and store employees pulled up beside me.

"Can't. Got to get to work," said a spindly guy driving a pickup. He gathered up his apron and jogged into the hardware store.

"Yeah, I'll be back in a few," said another guy. He looked honest enough, wearing a blue baseball cap with a green trout on it. So I watched his white four-door for awhile, but he never came back.

Finally it was almost ten, and no one else had passed by for a long time. I looked down the road to the Chevron station. They'd charge me for a boost, and I had only sixteen cents left in my pocket—heck, that was all I had left in the world. Then I heard the distant rumble of a big Ford truck. It was rolling slowly down the road, so I jumped in front of the girl driving. She screeched to a halt and rolled down her window.

"Please," I said. "I need a boost. I've got the cables. No one will help me, and I've got to get home. Please."

She turned around in her seat and glanced down the

road behind her, then she stared at a clock in her cracked dashboard, and then she finally said, "Okay. I'm late for work anyway."

Within a few minutes I was back on the perimeter loop of the city, heading toward home. I told myself to relax. I still had plenty of time if I didn't break down or run out of gas or—gas! I hadn't checked the tank. Matt usually ran on empty. Full to him was three bucks worth or an eighth of a tank, whichever came first. My gaze dropped slowly to the gas gauge. It was below empty, bouncing up and down with each dip in the road. Arrrggh!

I slowed to conserve fuel. There was no place to stop for gas even if I had the money, so I rode on fumes, or less than fumes—the car was running on the slimy green lining of Matt's gas tank. But the red Duster refused to die. Maybe it really did want to know how this was going to turn out.

It was well after ten-thirty when I pulled onto our road. The Duster had traveled miles with an empty gas tank, but as I made the turn into our driveway the engine began to make unnatural noises. The engine thudded and wheezed louder than our school's marching band. Finally it spat, lagged, then died. I opened the door and pushed the car to its usual resting place.

Sweet Pea was at the fence watching me. Even she wanted to be involved in the morning's events. I threw her a little hay and dashed into the house.

"Where in the world did you go at seven in the morning?" said a familiar voice.

I stopped dead at the foot of the stairs. Mom was standing in the kitchen door pointing her checkbook at me like a loaded gun. I'd torn into the house so fast I hadn't even noticed her truck in the driveway.

"I . . . er . . ." My mind raced for any possibility that would satisfy her cynical mind. The truth? Never! But close to the truth, that would work.

"Matt was left here stranded," she added. "I had to

give him a ride to the IGA." Matt bagged groceries on Saturdays.

"He knew I was gonna use the car," I managed to say, stalling while I thought up something creative. "Uh, I'm just doing something for the game tonight. Helping with the decorations."

"Are you serious?" She grabbed the door molding and started tapping a finger. "Don't you have enough to worry about as a player?"

"It's no big deal."

She rolled her eyes, shook her head, and lowered her checkbook. "I don't know."

"Serious. I don't mind."

"So what time is the game?"

"Why?"

"We want to come, that's why. What time do you play?" She was getting mad.

"Who's we? Who's coming? You and Dad? And Matt?"

"Yes, we're all coming. Are you embarrassed to have us in the stands? This *is* a pretty big game, you know."

Of course I knew. It was the biggest game in Spring Valley history. If we won this game, we'd make the state playoffs for the first time in years. I realized I couldn't stop them from coming, but that didn't mean I was excited about my mom and dad seeing my banner unfurl.

Still, what could I do?

"No, I don't care if you come." Anyway, I needed her truck now that Matt's car was out of gas. "But can I use your truck this afternoon? I've got this really big sign I need to haul to school. And Matt's car's out of gas."

"No, I'm going to work. I'm leaving right now," she said.

"Pleeease." I was getting desperate.

"I've got to get to work," she said. She looked at the hall telephone. "Maybe . . . let me call Mrs. Thomas and see if she'll take you in her pickup."

"Geez. I don't want her to take me."

"I don't think you have much choice."

Mom picked up the phone and called. Mrs. Thomas was home, but that was no surprise. Mrs. Thomas was always home. She was retired from the post office, and she hardly ever left her little farm house. Even in the winter I think she was worried that if she left for more than a few hours her Border collies would burn the place down or her farm would need some immediate attention she couldn't give it.

While I was waiting for Mrs. Thomas, I painted the letters of the sign in big, swirling red loops. I even added a couple of little hearts with our initials in them. I dried it with Mom's hair dryer and then packed the sign and all the wires in a potato sack.

I waited the rest of the morning and most of the afternoon for Mrs. Thomas. But she didn't pull into our driveway until the winter sun was getting low on the horizon. By that time I was past nervous—I was almost insane with worry. I had only a couple of hours before the game.

I knew she was finally coming when I heard her horn blaring up the road. Mrs. Thomas hadn't hit the horn. Her yellow pickup's horn had a mind of its own. It would blast at any time without warning. Almost every person in Spring Valley had at one time or another put his or her head under Mrs. Thomas's pickup hood, looking for the cause of the mysterious horn blasts. No one had ever figured it out. Even the mechanics in town had no idea what was causing it. Still, Mrs. Thomas didn't want the horn unplugged. She'd rather put up with the unscheduled blasts than go without a warning system.

The truck rounded the corner and pulled into our drive.

I ran to the door and jumped down the front stairs. Mrs. Thomas turned off the truck before it could honk again. Then she got slowly out of the cab and stuck her hands in her coveralls as if she were getting settled in for a long conversation.

"Your mother says you've got some program at school," she said, nodding her head slowly as she talked. As usual, Mrs. Thomas had a crabby look on her face. As far as I knew, she had never smiled. And she had deep wrinkles in her forehead, probably from years of worry that the mail wouldn't get delivered or that her half-dozen cows would get out.

"Uh, yeah, a game," I answered.

"Don't know why they need programs at school. If you ask me, they've got too many programs. You know what adjectives are? Verbs? Probably not. That's what we studied when I was in school. We got thirty minutes of calisthenics a day, leapfrog, rope climbing. Can you imagine me doing leapfrog? I don't know that I even remember how. Here, you lean over and I'll leapfrog you." She made a motion for me to lean over.

"You serious?" I asked.

She grunted. "No. I was pulling your leg. They don't teach you how to laugh, either. I'm not about to jump over you. What do you think my bones are made of?"

She kept talking while I rocked back and forth from one leg to the other. Actually, she was pretty funny in a weird sort of way, but I didn't have time to visit. Finally I cut in and asked, "Do you want me to get my stuff now?"

"Unless it can get itself."

I snickered nervously. "No."

I threw my bundle in the back of the truck before I felt my first pangs of guilt. I wasn't helping decorate at school. What if Mom and Dad got mad when they found out I was lying just to impress a girl? Still, what could I do?

"Thanks again," I said to Mrs. Thomas as she closed the back of the pickup.

"Egh," she kind of answered.

Sweet Pea turned her head and looked over at me. She let out a powerful snort and whinny. I smiled and climbed into Mrs. Thomas's truck, clutching my gym bag with my basketball uniform.

We pulled out onto the main road, and I lost sight of my house. Mrs. Thomas's yellow truck let out a harsh *honnnk,* and we accelerated toward the school.

— CHAPTER 11 —

My Banner Year

Mrs. Thomas pulled her pickup past the school to the back loading ramp. The truck's honking scared off a few birds that were living on the roof, but otherwise the place was quiet. The only car in the entire parking lot belonged to Wally Kellogg, the custodian.

"Thanks," I said, pulling the potato bag with the banner and assorted wires out of the pickup bed. "I couldn't have lugged this stuff by myself. Without a truck, I mean."

"What's in the bag?" she asked.

"Just a sign," I mumbled.

"Just a sign? What's it say?"

"Nothing. Just for the game, I guess."

Mrs. Thomas had lived by us for more than a dozen years, but just then she did something I had never seen her do before. She leaned out her window, took a good long look at the bag, and then actually broke into a smile. A big, broad grin.

"I was young once, myself," she said. "I still remember what it's like to be in love."

"How?" was all I could spit out, but she wasn't listening. She turned the key, the honking yellow pickup roared to life, and slowly she drove off.

How did she know what I had in the bag? It was strange, but I didn't have time to think about it.

I threw the bag onto the dumpster, and it landed with a loud *clang*. Too loud? I waited to see if Wally would come out, but he didn't. So I threw the bag onto the roof and pulled myself up after it. Most of the gym's upper windows were cracked open, probably to let the place ventilate. I chose a window over the south end. I quickly pushed in the bag and then dropped after it. I landed forty feet off the ground on a narrow steel beam.

I dropped to my knees and then my stomach and held tight.

Soon my hands were squirting sweat so badly I couldn't hang on. My legs were so weak I was afraid they would melt and slide off the beam.

Heights again!

"You have to move," I finally told myself. "Be tough. Be tough." I chanted.

Slowly I loosened my grip and inched along the beam toward the middle of the gym and away from the security of the open window. About a mile below me were the bleachers where Jeanette McCaffrey would sit. I kept inching along. It probably took half an hour, but I finally came to a point directly above the foul line of the south basket. I loosened the top of the sack and began working.

———

When Wally Kellogg opened the wide doors to the main entrance and the first parents and teachers started wandering in, I was still hanging onto the rafters. Working with one hand at that height was taking a lot longer than I had imagined.

From my perch I could see Principal Walker stride through the entrance. I could just imagine what he'd do if he saw me up there. He'd probably throw one of his shiny leather shoes at me to knock me off the beam. He thought I was an idiot anyway, ever since I flapped my arms in front of the Scout ceremony. He certainly would never let me unfurl my banner.

Finally all I had to do was attach the long, thin wire to the banner and then run it down to the ground. When I pulled on the wire, it would pull the banner off the beam. The banner would drop, unfurl, and—well, Jeanette would probably faint with excitement. This would be much better than being in a stupid book.

I started inching my way back along the beam to the open window, letting my spool of wire unravel as I went. It was a lot harder moving backward.

I looked down again, this time at the metal door that led to the team locker room. I was supposed to be getting into my basketball uniform about now. Someone would notice I wasn't there, probably. And if I didn't move faster, someone would definitely notice me on the beam. I had to move faster.

So I held my breath and pushed myself a full arm length. I was still alive, so I did it again, and again.

On the ground, the bleachers were beginning to fill. In the first row I saw Tom and Gwen Daugherty, in the third I saw Joe's parents, and in the fourth row I saw Paul and Leona Burhold, surrounded by locals telling their stories. And Paul had my binoculars around his neck. Arrrgh!

I moved again, pushing backward until my feet bumped into the back wall.

By the time I got off the roof and hid the wire behind the dumpster at the back of the school, the rest of my team was out on the court warming up. From the stuffy, smelly locker room, I could hear the rising voices of the crowd. I pulled on my shorts and then my sweats, then I raced out.

Sitting on the bench tying my high-tops, I watched Tony effortlessly slamming the ball through the south basket. Sometimes he did a three-sixty before he dunked.

Other times he pushed the ball around his back before jamming it through the rim. His third trick was slamming backwards. And every time he dunked, the crowd erupted with a deafening roar.

I scanned the crowded bleachers for Jeanette's face. It took a while to find her pack of friends near the top row, and then eventually I saw Jeanette and my heart squeezed to a stop.

Like everyone in the gym, she was watching Tony with eyes of wonder. It was time. I had to drop the banner. I jumped up and turned back toward the lockers, but then I felt a firm hand grab my arm.

"Where d'ya think you're going?" bellowed Coach. He was leaning close to my ear so he could be heard over the crowd as it again roared its approval of Tony Burhold. I tried to squirm away, but Coach tightened his grip on my arm.

"Uh, bathroom," I said. "Gotta go."

"Nerves," he said, laughing and letting go his grip.

I raced through the lockers and out the back door, out into the cold evening. In my haste I almost bumped into Randy Wallace, who was leaning against the dumpster smoking. Randy was in my English class. He was little and stumpy but mean as a weasel. He saw me in my uniform and started laughing.

"You gonna play out here?" he said through his nose, which was as big and bumpy as an Idaho potato.

"Not now, Randy," I said back.

"You scared, wimp?" I should have known he'd say something like that. He was always looking for a fight.

"I don't have time for this."

"You afraid?"

By this time, however, my mind had become incredibly adept at thinking up lies. "No," I said. "Some rich guy lost his wallet out in the front parking lot. I'm supposed to keep people in the building while he looks for it."

I didn't have to say any more. Randy was already sprinting up the loading ramp, heading toward the cars.

The wire was still dangling behind the dumpster. I pulled and felt the banner give. Then I let go and hoped by the time I got back to the gym the banner would be unfurled.

I don't know what I expected to happen upon my entrance. I suppose I wanted the students and parents of Spring Valley High to stand as a body and cheer as I ran in. I would raise my arms in triumph. I supposed I could have lived even through laughter.

But no. I was ignored.

I looked up to the south basket. No banner. I looked higher and higher—and there was the banner. It had started to fall, all right, but had tangled around the beam. It was a mess. There was absolutely no way it was coming down.

The buzzer sounded, and I dropped onto the far end of our bench.

"You didn't even warm up," said Joe, walking off the floor and patting me on the shoulder.

"Bathroom," I said again pathetically, trying to pull my eyes down from the tangled banner.

"Nerves," said Joe.

Joe and I took our seats on the bench, and the ref walked the ball to the middle of the floor for the tip-off. It was only then that I realized I *did* need to use the bathroom, really badly.

But then the game began.

I hadn't yet noticed Lewiston on the floor. But there they were, four thin guys with baggy shorts and one big ape. The ape guy was as tall as Tony and maybe even wider. He looked like he might bite someone's ear off if it got too close, so as the backup center I decided I wouldn't get within biting range if I got off the bench.

Spring Valley had the ball, and everyone was moving, jockeying for position around the north basket. Our team scored, but Lewiston's big guy scored right back. The teams raced back and forth, the heavy thud of the basket-

114

ball resounding off the hardwood and lifting high into the stands. But the sound met the yells of the people of Spring Valley and was muffled. Even the people I love—Mom, Dad, Matt, Jeanette—were yelling, "Shoot, Tony, shoot!" or "Deeefense!"

But this game proved to be much different than the one in Glasgow. The minutes flew by and Tony tried everything, but the long, hairy arms of the Lewiston player kept getting in the way. Tony was more athletic than the ape guy, but the ape guy was playing hard and smart. He seemed to be able to anticipate Tony's every move.

———

The ball bounced out of bounds with a minute left. Lewiston was up by three points. Joe and I, who had both sat on the bench the entire game, were leaning forward and nervously gripping the edge of the wooden bench as if we were on a porch swing that was flying through the air out of control.

The ball was thrown in at about midcourt, and my teammate Wayne controlled it, bringing it slowly up court. He looked inside to Tony but changed his mind and dribbled back outside. A smart move. Tony was as cold as frozen fish sticks.

Wayne dribbled just outside the three-point circle until Greg broke free inside. Wayne didn't hesitate. He fired a bullet of a pass through traffic. Greg bounced the ball with his left hand and then laid a soft shot off the backboard that dropped into the net. The crowd erupted.

We were all on our feet by then. I was gripping a towel and ringing it with my hands.

Still up by one, Lewiston stalled, bringing the ball up court slowly to kill time. Fifteen seconds later they started looking for a shot, but our defense boxed them out. When they finally got a poor shot off, it bounced off the rim and Tony was able to pull it down and tuck it under his chest.

Again the crowd went wild as Spring Valley dashed for the south basket.

I looked up at the clock. Twenty seconds, nineteen, eighteen—

Wayne was again outside the three-point line, waiting, bobbing back and forth, looking for an opening. Ten seconds, nine, eight, seven, six, five—Everyone in the crowd was yelling, screaming at the top of their lungs for Wayne to shoot, to pass, to do something. They were pounding on the bleachers, screaming, shaking the entire building so hard I imagined the roof might come down.

"Shoot!" I yelled as loud as I could, but my voice was lost amid the frenzy and the foot-stomping of the crowd. I was so wound up I didn't even notice what was happening above us.

And then Tony was open for a split second behind the three-point line and to the right of the basket. Wayne saw him and pushed the ball over. Without squaring up, Tony jumped high, and as if in slow motion he let the ball fly just as the buzzer sounded and just as my banner, shaken loose by the crowd, floated down and down to a point directly in front of the south basket.

Jeanette, be mine forever! Andrew

Tony's shot tore through the paper and everyone—the players, the ref, the crowd—watched as the ball fell dead to the ground. The ball didn't even make it to the basket. It bounced a few times before coming to a rest by someone's foot.

Tony's shot had removed the middle of the banner.

Jeanette, be Andrew, it now read.

No one said anything. But person by person, the crowd turned its stunned attention from the banner to me. Even Joe looked over his shoulder, absolutely amazed. But still no one said anything.

Then the ref, figuring out where the crowd's attention was focused, walked over to the bench.

"That your banner, son?" he asked me.

"Um, yes, sir," I said.

The ref turned around and started waving his arms. "No basket, no basket. Lewiston wins!" he yelled at the collective players.

Coach ran out onto the court to fight the call, and our players swarmed after him, but I had lost interest by that point. I looked up into the stands. I saw my mom and dad, Matt and his friends, the Daughertys, the Burholds, Principal Walker, everyone. And then I found Jeanette. Jeanette McCaffrey, the girl I had hoped to impress with my greatest show of creativity, was sitting with her face in her hands, embarrassed—no mortified—by my idiotic gesture.

Coach was coming back off the floor, rubbing his shiny scalp. He was probably wondering if he could kill me and still keep his job. He was followed by my teammates. Now they were all walking toward me, and they looked very, very mad.

But behind them, still under the banner, stood Tony. And Tony Burhold wore the only smile in the crowd. Tony knew I was finished, ruined. Maybe he wasn't as dumb as I'd thought.

It's not too late to run, my fevered mind thought. *Just run and keep running until you get to Canada.*

But before I could move, and before Coach and the angry team could reach me, Principal Walker had regained enough of his cool to realize the idiot Andrew Stenson had struck again. So in his patent-leather shoes, he sprang down from the bleachers still full of stunned spectators and sprinted toward me.

Before I had time to move, Principal Walker reached me and grabbed both my arms. His face was past red; it was blue and crisscrossed with purple veins I'd never noticed before.

"What could you possibly have been thinking?" he yelled at me, speaking the first complete sentence I had ever heard him utter. "You insane, man?"

117

I started to answer. I wanted to answer, but he cut me off. "Don't . . . say . . . anything," he spat, enunciating each word with crisp diction.

His face was so blue, so hot, I thought the top of his head might pop off at any moment. Actually, I hoped it would, just to take the attention off me and my stupid banner.

He spun me around and pushed me by the shoulders the length of the basketball court, toward the front doors.

During that long walk, I lifted my eyes just a few times. Each time I met the eyes of someone I knew, someone who at that moment hated me. And finally, the last people I remember seeing on that long walk were Paul and Leona Burhold.

Leona was pointing at me and saying something while Paul scribbled furiously in his little notebook.

— CHAPTER 12 —

A Room with a View

That night I walked home. I didn't feel the cold because my body was warm from humiliation. At the house I slipped in the back way, ran upstairs, and locked the door to my room. Mom and Dad knocked at about eleven, a kind, quiet knock, but I didn't answer.

Long into the night I ran the events of the past few months over and over in my mind. And the more the events unfolded, the worse I felt. In my quest to impress Jeanette, I'd spent all my money, lied to my family, and let down my team and my school.

By Sunday morning I had decided to never leave my room again. I could finish school by correspondence. By Sunday night I was making plans to run away—to Mexico maybe. But on Monday morning I knew what I had to do: face up to what I'd done.

I left home early, very early, and walked to school before any other kids got there. When I reached Principal Walker's office, Mrs. Lansing, the office secretary, looked up from her desk, shook her head, and pointed to a chair in the principal's waiting room. Mrs. Lansing's area was separated from the waiting room by a glass wall, so I couldn't hear what she was saying to herself. But I could see her grab her pad and pencil and make some notes, probably for my permanent record. *Andrew Stenson's hormones lost us the most important basketball game in school history.*

Mr. Walker didn't get there for another half hour. When he finally showed up, I was pacing in front of his office door. I tried to smile at him, but he obviously wasn't in the mood to be friendly.

"Sit there. Don't move!" he told me, pointing to the chair closest to his door. He stopped and checked his pant pockets. Then he walked out and around the glass partition to Mrs. Lansing's side. I held my breath to listen.

"Carol, my good suit? Meeting with school board at two," I heard him say, as if she were his wife—or mother.

"You took your suit home last week," she said. "It needed cleaning."

Principal Walker thumped the counter. Oh, geez. His mood would not be improved by having to wear those blue polyester slacks to a meeting with the school board. He probably had the most unattractive legs of any man in Spring Valley anyway. But the blue slacks he was wearing made him look like he was walking on stilts.

He walked back around the glass wall, then through the waiting room to his office. He slammed his door, and I was left alone, looking at Mrs. Lansing on the other side of the glass wall. She again shook her head at me and went back to her paperwork.

By then the school was filling. And on their way to classes, it seemed most of the student body walked by the principal's waiting room. I sat there looking pathetic. Every single person looked in. And most made some sort of threat, even the ninth-graders. The guys from my team made threats, people from my classes, everyone. To them I had become the world's biggest loser.

Matt was the first person to actually stop. He looked from side to side and then walked in.

"You know—" was all he got out, and then he started to laugh his characteristic "Ha, ha, ha—snort." Then he patted my shoulder and sat beside me. "It's actually kind of funny."

I looked at him with as much hatred as my beaten soul could muster. Laughter was the last thing I expected out of anyone for a long time. "Shuddup," I said. "Just shuddup."

"Aw, you can't get rid of me that easy," he said. "I'll stick with you. I've been in here a few times myself."

"Gee, thanks," I grunted. But I did appreciate Matt's support, especially since he blocked me from the view of the never-ending stream of jerks passing in the hallway.

A few minutes later I leaned forward and dared to look out into the hall again. Jeanette's pack of friends was passing by. They looked in and whispered to each other. They were too embarrassed for Jeanette to say anything mean to me, though I knew they wanted to. To them I was a humiliating geek who had disgraced their coolness.

And then Jeanette walked by. I started to stand up and motion to her, but I felt Mrs. Lansing's glare cut through the glass wall like a Star Trek phaser. I sat back into the plastic chair.

Jeanette knew I was in the office waiting room, but she didn't even look. She seemed to walk by in slow motion, never turning or acknowledging I was there. And then she was gone, out of sight of the waiting-room doorway. Gone. Forever.

I let out a little whimper, and Matt again patted my shoulder.

Then Tony Burhold filled the wide doorway. He looked right in and slowly, ever so slowly, the edges of his mouth started rising and rising until his smile was as wide as his head. He was quite tickled that I'd become the biggest bum in Spring Valley history. If my banner hadn't fallen and his shot had missed, he'd be the loser right then.

Then, as a final measure of supremacy, Tony called after Jeanette and began to jog down the hallway to her.

"That jerk!" I said, thumping my leg.

"Oh, give it up," said Matt. "Even *you* have to realize by now that Jeanette's a lost cause."

But no, even then I didn't want to believe it.

"If Tony hadn't moved to town, everything would've been fine," I said. "Jeanette and I would be going out."

"Maybe you're forgetting. The only reason you asked Jeanette out was to get to her before Tony. If he hadn't moved to town, you'd still be staring at her with misty eyes."

"Shuddup."

I didn't want to hear Matt's psychological abstract of my misery. I'd just spent the past two months and all my money impressing a girl who, during my hour of need, had just walked by without even caring.

"I took her for a balloon ride," I said. "Ice sculpting. We went on a chase in Dad's squad car. I mean, any girl would die to do that kind of stuff. Wouldn't she?"

"How should I know? I guess you were doing a pretty good job impressing her—until now, I mean. But, maybe you should have found out if she really liked you before you spent all your money and—er, energy."

We sat in silence waiting for Principal Walker, who I hoped was cooling down in his blue polyester slacks.

"Maybe you went a little crazy," Matt said. "Lied, spent too much money, tried too—"

"All right, I get the point!"

"But at least you tried," added Matt.

I looked up at him and nodded my head. "I did take the best-looking girl in school out, at least a few times."

"Yeah," said Matt. "And every girl in school knows who you are now."

I buried my head in my hands. Uggh.

But as I sat there, it gradually sank in. Matt was right; I had gone insane. Over the past few weeks, I had lost sight of the most important question a guy should ask in such a situation. Did Jeanette really like me for who I was?

I had spent all my money and time trying to impress her. And why? Because she was good-looking, because she was popular.

But in a strange way, it was comforting now that it was decided, now that I thought I knew the difference between love and infatuation.

"Hmmm," said Matt in an interested way. I brought my head up and followed his stare out into the hallway.

She was obviously a new girl. A blond new girl. Not Jeanette McCaffrey gorgeous, but cute. Really cute. She was walking into Mrs. Lansing's office, turning her head a lot and looking up and down the halls as if she was nervous or really needed to find the bathroom. She was with a woman I guessed was her mother. Even the girl's mother still looked pretty good, though she was at least forty.

Matt looked over at me. "No!" he said, amazed at my continuing stupidity. "Don't even think about it. Stay away from her, from all girls, for at least a few years. Until you're twenty-one. Maybe even thirty."

What did he know?

By that time the girl's mother was talking with Mrs. Lansing. Mrs. Lansing pushed some form at the mother, who leaned over and started filling it out. Obviously she was enrolling the girl in school. Obviously she would have to write the girl's name on the form. If I could just see that form . . .

"Are you dense?" Matt whispered to me as I crept across the waiting-room floor to the glass wall. "Walker'll be out any second!"

I put my index finger to my lips. "Shhhh. Watch Walker's door."

He responded by shaking his big melon head and rolling his eyes.

I had to stand on the tips of my toes to see over the mother's shoulder. Every now and then she would move, and I would get a glimpse of the penciled name at the top of the form. It definitely began with a C. Or was it a G? I pressed my face tighter against the glass wall. I couldn't think of a girl's name beginning with G. Maybe Gretchen? She was no Gretchen. Had to be a C.

I pushed even tighter to the glass, squashing my face. It was a C, and then—almost, yes, a B—no, it couldn't be a B. I had almost got it, almost, when I heard the creak of a door and Matt's cough.

"Andrew Stenson! You stupid idiot!" bellowed Principal Walker at the top of his lungs.

Just then the new girl and her mother spun around to see my distorted eyeball and smashed face pressed against the office's glass wall. And I still hadn't got her name.

That's how I met Cathy Connor.

Chapter 13

The Meaning of Life
at the IGA

I am having the dream again.

I'm wearing my basketball uniform, playing in a game in the school gym. I'm dribbling effortlessly around players like they're statues. I've never played this well before. But suddenly the gym gets dark, and I'm bouncing the ball in a crowd of people who are dressed for a prom. The other players are gone, and I notice everyone else is dancing. I'm still in my gym shorts, bouncing, bouncing, bouncing the ball.

Dancing in front of me is a girl in a blue silk dress, her hair piled loosely on her head. The rush of the crowd bumps me up against her, and she turns around. It's Jeanette. She takes my breath away, and I cannot speak.

Jeanette recognizes me and smiles, squeezes my arm. But then she laughs and slaps the ball away from me. It bounces up the court, weaving between dancers, until it is picked up under the basket by Tony. Tony is wearing a black tux with a Mickey Mouse bow tie. He puts the ball under his arm and then points his finger into the air like a disco dancer.

Then he tries to dribble, but the ball hits the floor with a plop. It's flat. He faces me and is furious.

"You broke it!" he yells. Others start shouting at me, even Jeanette. I'm scared, frantic.

"I didn't do it," I say, but everyone knows I'm lying.

I try to run off the court, but now there are high brick walls where the bleachers should be. Tony is struggling to push through the crowd to get to me. Hands grab at me, but I twist away from them and take off like a rock from a slingshot. Then I see an opening in the wall, and I run into it and am alone.

———

It's been five months since the game.

This morning the dream woke me, as usual. My eyes opened slowly, and I saw it was light but well before my alarm was scheduled to make its obnoxious noise. I didn't want to go back to sleep after that; not to a dream where I'm still a liar and where Tony is waiting for me. So I dropped out of bed and pulled on my work clothes.

Outside it was a cool, dewy summer morning. I breathed in, and it smelled familiar: it was the smell of our wet soccer field during early-morning practices.

I grabbed my water jug and then got Dad's shovel and pick from the garage. Shouldering the tools, I set out over the long grass to the back of Mrs. Thomas's farm, walking into the morning breeze toward the long line of brown hills dotted with aspen.

Summer was now well underway. Eleventh grade was a distant memory. And there was no one out in Mrs. Thomas's field who knew about the banner. In fact, there usually was no one out on the fence line at all except me.

As I planted the day's first steel fence post, I hit a rock. I pulled the post out, raised the pick, and swung at the hole, letting the weight of the pick lift me off the ground. There was a sharp crack as the metal edge splintered the rock on one edge. I pulled the pick out of the hole and prepared to strike again, but this time I flexed my developing forearms as I lifted the wooden handle. I had been building Mrs. Thomas's new fence for only a few weeks, but the work was already building muscles in my arms and shoulders.

I chipped through the rock, planted the post, and moved another eight feet to do it again. All morning I moved along, enjoying the repetition, the isolation, the growing heat.

Then I noticed Mrs. Thomas and her collies behind me.

"What's the poop?" she asked somberly, tugging at the post I'd just planted.

"Why? What's wrong?" I asked defensively. I wiped my forehead and then walked toward her and studied the bottom of the post.

"Nothing. Can't do much wrong sticking in a post," she said. "I just saw you out here early this morning, before I goosed the cows." That's what she called milking.

I shrugged and squatted down to scratch her dogs. "I don't know. Just couldn't sleep."

"Mornings are for the young," she said.

"I don't know about that. This morning, maybe."

"When my son, Bob, was young, he got up early. Most days he used the bathroom and went right back to bed. But to his credit, he did get up early."

I laughed.

"But you know, Bob went swimming in the afternoon, at the pool in town. I don't know why you don't go to town and have a swim."

Going swimming in this heat sounded good. But the thought of being seen in Spring Valley enjoying myself made the hair stand up on the back of my neck. "Uh, no. That's okay. I reckon in town I'd be about as popular as zits."

"What's zits?"

"You know, zits. Pimples. Acne."

"Oh. Well, suit yourself," she said. "But you're working so fast you'll be out of a job soon."

We looked toward the east fence. I hadn't noticed I was so close to finishing the new line.

"You see the paper yesterday?" Mrs. Thomas asked, raising her eyebrows.

"No."

"They had a write-up on them Burholds. Seems they've finished their book about—"

"Spring Valley," I said.

"Uh, no. Said they started out writing about the town, but then they got this idea to try to write about why teenagers do such embarrassing stuff to impress each other."

"What?"

"Yeah. I wonder where they got the idea for that?" she said, giving me one of her rare smiles.

"Ugh!" I said. Another reason to dread the twelfth grade.

She took a few paces toward the east fence. "About ten, maybe eleven more posts and we'll be ready to string line."

I nodded sadly.

"We better get some fencing today," she said. "I can't go. I have to watch the house." She reached into her overall pocket and pulled out her car keys, holding them up and jingling them in front of me like a baby rattle.

"You go," she said, handing me the keys.

I didn't move to take them. "Go where?" I asked.

"To town. I have a list of things I need."

"But—" I sputtered, but I couldn't continue. I couldn't say no to Mrs. Thomas. I took the keys from her wrinkled hand, and we began to walk together.

"When I was your age," she was saying, "we went on treasure hunts in the summer. We knocked on all the neighbors' doors and told them we needed things like molasses or sugar or flour. And then when we got back home we baked a cake." I laughed at that, but I wasn't really paying attention to her story. I was worried about heading into town, worried about my face being on the cover of the Burholds' teenage book. Just worried.

———

By the time I pulled Mrs. Thomas's honking yellow pickup into the IGA parking lot, it was almost noon. I had the fence wire in the back of the truck, but I needed to get Mrs. Thomas's groceries.

I parked well away from the building and walked in with my ball cap pulled down over my face. I checked Mrs. Thomas's list and rounded up the easy items. Milk was in the back, bread in the front, chicken along the far wall. But then she'd written *soup stock for chicken.* What was soup stock? I looked around and then up at a store directory dangling from the ceiling. *Soup, row 4.* Must be there.

No one had seen me yet because I was moving fast. But when I spun around the aisle end, I just about knocked over Matt, who was in his red IGA apron pricing soup cans. He quickly raised his price gun to protect himself.

"Watch where you're pointing that thing, Tex," I said.

He pointed at a fresh price sticker on one of the soup cans. "Yeah, you're not worth sixty-nine cents."

I pulled off the sticker and rubbed it into a ball.

"Thought you said you weren't coming into town this summer," said Matt.

"I'm not staying long," I replied. "Just got to get some stuff for Mrs. Thomas. Where's the soup stock?"

"How should I know?"

"Gee, I wonder why they haven't made you manager yet."

We scanned the shelves for chicken soup stock.

"Mrs. Thomas wanted me to go swimming at the pool," I said, expecting Matt to share my amazement.

He chuckled but didn't comment.

"I bet this is the stuff," he said, pulling down a yellow cylinder from a top shelf. He blew a layer of dust off the top of the container.

"Don't get much call for it, huh?" I asked.

"Guess not." He checked the expiration date. "Hey, it's still good."

He walked me to the end of the aisle. "You'll never guess who's working here," Matt said.

"Good or bad?"

"Depends."

"Tony Burhold?" I asked, feeling my chest tighten.

"Nope.

"Not Jeanette?"

"Nope."

Relief. "Who?"

"The girl you eyed up in Principal Walker's office."

"Cathy Connor?"

"Yup."

Down at the registers, Cathy was ringing up some guy's pop and chips. She was the only cashier.

"Great. Isn't anyone else working the registers?" I asked as the tightness in my chest returned.

"I don't think so."

"Pay for my stuff," I whined.

"And miss seeing you squirm? No way."

"Jerk."

"Loser."

————

"Hi," said Cathy brightly.

"Yeah, hi," I grunted back, pushing my items toward her so I didn't have to wait for the conveyor belt.

She picked up the squishy chicken package and punched the price into the register.

"You're Matt's brother, aren't you?" she said, looking up at me.

I could have lied then, but I was through with lying.

"Yeah, I guess." I kept my eyes fixed on the chicken soup stock as she picked it up.

"This sure is dusty." She ran her finger around the top of the container. Then she punched in the price.

"You're not very talkative," said Cathy, stopping and looking directly at me. I had to raise my face and look at her. She had her lips pressed together in a funny sort of grin.

"Look. Just go ahead and laugh," I said. "I'm used to it."

"What?"

"Laugh. Call me an idiot. I don't care."

"It's just dusty soup stock. It's no big deal." She held up the can and tilted it, letting a little of the dust fall onto the produce scale.

"No. I mean you can laugh about my banner."

"Oh, that thing at the basketball game? Marci told me. I think it's funny."

"Yeah, funny."

"No, not that kind of funny. I think it's cute. I wish some guy would do something like that for me."

"No you don't, I promise."

She smiled. "I remember you," she said, leaning forward, "from the day I enrolled at school."

My face blushed instantly. "Oh, brother."

"You made that funny face on the glass. It made me laugh. It even made my mom laugh. I needed to laugh that day. I'd never changed schools before."

"I didn't know you laughed. Walker was pretty mad at me."

She rang up the milk. I pushed my ball cap back on my head.

"So where'd you move from?" I asked.

"Idaho."

"Oh, I'm sorry."

"Har, har. Very funny. It's nice there." She reached across the conveyor belt and slugged my shoulder, then giggled.

"I guess."

"It *is*."

There weren't any customers waiting in line. I had Cathy Connor all to myself, for a few minutes anyway. So I thought up something else to ask.

"You like working here?"

"Yeah, everybody's nice. And Matt's really funny."

"My brother, Matt?"

"Yes."

"Funny?"

"He *is*."

I smiled and nodded. "Yeah, he's pretty funny, I guess. Sometimes."

We talked and joked, and while we did something slowly seeped into my brain: Cathy Connor seemed to like me. She seemed to like me in spite of the stupid stuff I did. And best of all, she didn't care about the banner!

I had spent the past five months convinced that every person in Spring Valley was obsessed with my dumb banner. But if Cathy didn't care, maybe the rest of Spring Valley had stopped caring. I had messed up a game, but after all, it was just a game.

"So you're almost done?" Cathy asked, saying it as if she'd asked the question a couple of times before.

I obviously had drifted off. I tried to concentrate. "Huh?"

"The fence?" she asked.

"Oh, yeah. We'll probably run the wire tomorrow or the next day," I said.

"Then what'll you do, for a job I mean?"

I answered, though I forget what I said because at that moment I looked up at the digital clock over the store entrance. The time was 12:17 P.M. And now, only hours later,

132

I recognize that was the minute my life began to move again, to accelerate.

———

The rest of my conversation with Cathy is kind of fuzzy, like scenes from one of my goofy dreams. I remember listening to her soft voice and laughing at the funny things she said. But most of all I remember it sinking in that it wasn't so tough after all being with a girl, talking, laughing, being myself.

And being myself, I finally realize, is what it's all about. That I don't have to be cooler or smarter or even more creative than I really am. If I be myself, I'll be more likeable, I won't have to lie, and maybe, just maybe, I'll fall in love one day.

I guess that's what I've always respected about Matt, that he doesn't pretend to be somebody he's not.

———

Matt came to the end of his aisle just then. He saw Cathy and me together, and he smiled, raising up his price gun like an extension of his fist, like a boxer after a fight.

I couldn't help laughing out loud at him. I leaned back on my feet, pulled off my ball cap, and let it fly in his direction, but a rush of warm air coming from outside caught the cap and lifted it above my brother.

Matt laughed, "Ha, ha, ha—snort." Then Cathy laughed too.

But in a second we were all quiet, staring open-mouthed as the cap seem to hang in midair over aisle four, over the dusty soup stock.

And you know, for a moment all my fears were suspended.

.

About the Author

Adrian Gostick began his writing career running a small-town newspaper in British Columbia, Canada. He has worked as a writer and editor for the *New Era* magazine and is still a frequent contributor. He now serves as assistant vice president and manager of communications and public relations for First Security Corporation in Salt Lake City.

Born in Burton, England, Adrian has lived in various parts of the United Kingdom and North America. He received a B.A. in journalism from Brigham Young University. Adrian lives in Oakley, Utah, with his wife and son.

Adrian's first novel for young adults, *Eddy and the Habs,* was published in 1994.